I Gave Him Loyalty, He Gave Me Lies:
Brandon & Tiff

By: Londyn Lenz

Brandon

"Why are you so quiet brown sugar? What'chu thinking about?" I laid in bed and wrapped my arms around my wife. I noticed she was quiet more than normal tonight. We had just put our daughter Brandy down to bed. Her little wild ass had been on speed all day, so she clocked out before 9 o'clock tonight. Me and Tiff took a shower and were now in bed watching TV, but I could tell her mind was somewhere else.

"I'm just thinking about our move. Brandon, we have been in Louisiana our whole life. I'm so nervous to start a new life in Miami." I looked down at my beautiful wife while she expressed her fears to me. I knew deep down her fear was the history I held in Miami. I sat up in the bed and pulled Tiff between my legs. She was sitting on her feet with her face in my face. I tilted her chin up, so she can look at me and see my sincerity.

Tiffany, talk to me and tell me how you are really feeling about this Miami move." I grabbed her hand and interlocked our fingers together.

"I don't know Brandon. You went there before and cheated on me. That shit almost destroyed us, what if you do it again? It's a lot of temptation in Miami especially when Spring break comes. It's scary Brandon." Her voice started to crack, and she blinked away the tears that were coming.

"Tiffany, I would never do that stupid shit to you again. I was on some little boy type of behavior. Now, look at us and how far we have come. We are married and have a beautiful little girl. I would never jeopardize our family for some ass. It's a lot of temptation here to but I push past that shit. You and Brandy are what matters and ain't no room for shit else. Now, give me some sugar brown sugar."

She smiled and brought her lips to mine.

I kissed my wife and the same feeling I got since we have been sixteen years old came to me. That heart pounding, blood rushing to one side butterfly feeling. And my dick felt some type of way as well. My wife was so pretty with her soft skin the color of brown sugar which is where I came up with her name. I gave her that nick name when I first laid eyes on her. Tiff has shoulder length hair that thanks to her mama has nice texture. One of my favorite features on my wife were her full ass lips. She had almond shaped brown eyes and a smile that lit up a dim ass room. Tiff was 5'7 with sexy ass legs and thighs.

Tiff's body used to be slim thick with a fat ass booty. But after she had our daughter Brandy, her hips have spread, her thighs and ass kept the extra baby weight. I was loving it and made sure I showed how much I was loving it every day. Kissing her made my king cobra come to life. She must have felt some type of way to because while still kissing me, she straddled my lap. Her hips were grinding on me and I felt her warm pussy against my dick. I had on some Polo boxers and no shirt. Pussy was on my mind so when Tiff pulled away I was confused about why she stopped.

"Brandon, I love you and I'm doing this move for us. Don't make me regret my decision." I looked at her and rubbed the side of her face. My eyes examined her entire face as my other hand rubbed her back.

"Tiffany, I got you. I swear on my life, I got you." I was done using my words to express how I was feeling. I unsnapped her bra she had on from the back. Freeing her pretty, bouncing titties with pierced nipples. I pulled away and looked at her pretty ass titties while biting my lip. Tiff had some of the prettiest titties I had ever seen. And that's including all the porn I have watched in my lifetime. Tiff had a sexy ass smirk on her face.

"Make my pussy sore daddy." Swear when she said that shit in her seductive tone, I almost exploded. I grabbed her by her neck and jammed my tongue down her throat. Tiff was sucking on my tongue and biting on my lip just like I loved. With my hand still around her throat I slammed her on her back and got on top of her. My force didn't hurt her, but it was enough for her to realize that I planned on doing exactly what she wanted. I was going to make that pussy ache and love this dick all in the same breath.

*

Tiff was sleeping peacefully next to me. I grabbed my phone and took a picture of my brown sugar. She looked so good sleeping, her hair was all over the place. Laying on her side she had her hands pressed together between her legs. The only time she slept that way was when I showed no mercy on that pussy of hers. We fucked like champs all the time! I'm telling you if we made a porno the shit would change anybody's life who watched it. We were into all kinds of wild shit, but we'll get more into that later on. I kissed my wife and slid out of bed to head to the bathroom. After releasing in the toilet and handling my stank ass breath, I headed to Brandy's room.

It was only 5am so I knew my squeak wasn't up yet. Walking into her room I always smiled for a few reasons. One of them being how Tiff had Brandy's bedroom set up. The colors were pink and black. Brandy's name was hanging from her pink sheer curtains in big pink glitter letters. She had heart shaped furniture and her bed was something for a queen instead of a 2-and-a-half-year-old. There were six black steps and on each step in pink cursive letters were words written on them. Beautiful, Fearless, Sweet, Love, Believe and Courageous. The steps led to her full-size bed with black and pink fury covers and pillows.

Brandy was in love with her room and she preferred it more than her play room. I stood over her bed and looked at her sleep. My squeak was so beautiful with pretty brown skin like her mama. Her hair was jet black and curly but her most beautiful feature was her eyes. They were big and dark just like mine. Looking at her was like looking at the innocent side of me. Tiff couldn't stand how much Brandy resembled me but I took pride in that shit. Brandy was a constant reminder of how blessed I was and how I almost risked not having any of this.

Almost four years ago me and my brothers decided to go to Miami for spring break. I wasn't going to go. Me and Tiff had plans to go to Myrtle Beach in South Carolina. But we had some huge argument two days before we were supposed to leave. Thinking back, I don't even remember what the argument was about. But me and Tiff are both stubborn and bullheaded when we are upset. She had packed some shit out of our condo we lived in at the time and went to stay with her parents. I was on some 'I don't give a fuck' type of shit and I let her go.

I decided to leave Tiff in Louisiana and go to Miami with my bros. This was before they had their ladies, so I knew the turn up was going to be real. I went down there with intentions on drinking, throwing money at strippers and laying out on the beach. Me, Karlos, Kalvin, Kevin and Kaylin owned a bad ass beach house in Miami. The shit was all white and sky blue with six-bedrooms, seven-bathrooms, a chrome and black kitchen topped off with a pool and sauna. Bitches loved that house and dropped the panties as soon as they walked in.

I had never been a weak nigga who couldn't keep his dick in his pants. Y'all read the other books about us so y'all are familiar with my bros. Bitches followed us where ever we went, that shit was just a given. No matter how bad the chick would be I never strayed on my brown sugar and any bitch who tried to get in my face knew that. I curved hoes more than my dick curved in Tiff's pussy. So, going to Miami and being around a bunch of loose hoes was not about to bother me.

We get down there and just like I expected, the turn-up was to the max. We were drunk every fuckin' night. Bought out club after club! The money we threw at strippers was enough to cover the mortgage, car payment and shopping sprees! One night we decided to throw a get together at our beach house. The Royals name spoke volumes anywhere we went. Mama Staci and Kaine took me in as their fifth child when I was seven years old, so I was a Royal in their eyes. I'll tell ya'll about my childhood later. Anyway, our party was packed and filled with bad bitches in swimsuits all through our shit.

We invited a few niggas from our crew and a few we fucked with whenever we were in Miami. Any event we threw always was drama free. An argument or two may start between a hoe yelling at another hoe, but that's as big as the drama would get. People knew not to fuck up our shit or that was their ass. So, I'm chillin' at the party when this brown skin thick chick in white swimsuit bottoms and a tight fishnet short top walks up on me. I ain't no blind nigga so I will admit the bitch was bad as fuck. She had these pouty lips and an angelic face. Almost like sugar and spice was used to make her bad ass.

The chick was bad as fuck and when she approached me in our pool we just talked it up. I learned her name was Blair and she had been in Miami for a year. We chopped it up in the pool for a bit. The conversation just flowed, and I told her off rip I had a girl and wasn't shit poppin' between me and her. After more conversation and more drinks, I ended up letting Blair suck my dick in one of our bedrooms. Now, between me and you the head was fire! But after I nutted I felt like shit. I had never cheated on Tiff before then.

I told Blair that what we did stays on the low. This

bitch reassured me that it was our secret and she would keep her lips sealed. We went back to the party and had a good ass time the rest of the night. My bros were smashing bitch after bitch especially Karlos' ass, he was on a fucking record. Blair was cool as fuck the rest of the party and after Miami, I planned on never seeing or hearing from her again. I had never been so wrong! That bitch followed me on Instagram and I didn't know it. My page was not private, so all my pics were public.

Blair had sent me some DMs asking if we could see each other again and she liked how we vibed. Any other time I would have seen what she was about because our convo was cool as fuck. But a fuckin' conversation would never make me want to start shit up with a bitch. Hell, me and Tiff had some good ass talks so that area wasn't lacking. I told Blair to stop sending me DMs and I blocked her ass. That's when I fucked up, that bitch DM Tiff and told her everything. She sent her our conversations about me threating her if she opens her mouth. That bitch went all out and made a fake account and everything. She told Tiff her name was Michelle and she sucked my dick in Miami. The DMs she had between me and her is what really fucked me up.

My brown sugar was so hurt. I begged and pleaded for her not to leave me but she wasn't trying to hear shit. She packed all her shit and moved out. I bought gifts after gifts of all kinds, but that shit didn't work. After a few months she started dating some lame ass nigga. I wanted to kill that muthafucka but I knew that would push Tiff away even more. I know my brown sugar better than she knows herself. So, I knew she was just dating that nigga to piss me off. He didn't even touch her pussy. He was simply a pawn in her getting back at me. It took six-months to get my brown sugar back.

And I would have waited longer if she made me.

Now, I wasn't squeaky clean while we were broken up. After four months I started smashin' bitches and nuttin' in their hair. I was so fucked up that I never went back to me and Tiff's condo. I slept in hotels and I never slept alone. Something about an empty bed and an empty room fucked with me. On the sixth month I went to get my brown sugar back.

I didn't have to snatch her from ol'boy because he was gone after three weeks of them dating. Like I said, he was just a pawn. Tiff forgave me and we have been together strong ever since. All that I put her through emotionally I was so blessed that she took me back. Now look at us, we were married and parents. I kissed my squeak on her cheek and left out her room. Walking down stairs I went to our kitchen and began to cook my family some breakfast. I loved cooking breakfast for Tiff. She handled lunch and dinner and I tackled breakfast. My pancakes and waffles were a homemade recipe my grandma made up when I was little. She taught me how to make them before she passed away.

My eggs were good as hell and so was my French toast and grits. Today, I was making waffles, eggs and turkey bacon. I was shirtless with my boxers and red apron mixing my waffle mix. Jay-Z's 4:44 album played through my Google speaker. While I put my next batch in the waffle iron I felt some arms wrap around my waist. Tiff started kissing me all over my back and them soft lips felt like pillows. I put the mixing bowl in the sink and turned around to kiss my wife.

"Good morning brown sugar. I see you still got that dick down glow on yo' face." I put my arms around her waist and squeezed her fat booty.

"That I do and now I'm ready for my husband to feed me." We kissed a little more and I went back to making our plates. Tiff went back upstairs and moments later she came back down holding Brandy.

"Daddy!" Her high squeaky voice bounced off the kitchen walls. I smiled big as hell as she jumped out of Tiff's arms and into mine.

"Good morning squeak, you love your daddy?" I asked while kissing all over her making her smile big and laugh.

"NO!" Brandy shouted smiling. Me and Tiff fell out laughing because she said no to any and everything you ask her.

"My squeak, you don't love daddy?" Tiff asked her smiling as I placed Brandy in her chair.

"NO!"

"Do you love me?" Tiff asked pointing to herself.

"NO!" Me and Tiff were cracking up which made Brandy laugh hard and squeak loudly.

"Do you love pop-pop and granny?"

"NO!"

"What about chocolate milk and bananas?" I asked because that was my squeak's favorite

"NOOOO!" Tiff smacked her lips laughing and I shook my head laughing. I placed our plates on the table and set down with my family. After we thanked God for our food we started eating.

"Are you hanging with the girls today?" I asked Tiff while she stuffed eggs in her mouth.

"Yup, me and Brandy are meeting them at Kylee's house. I know you and the guys are getting together." She asked me. I nodded and took a swig of my orange juice. Brandy was fuckin' her waffle up getting syrup all over her hands and mouth.

After we ate Tiff cleaned up the kitchen while I went and got me, and Brandy dressed. She had already laid out her clothes she wanted her to wear. Brandy had her own bathroom in her room, so I took her by the hand and gave her a bath. She played and laughed while I got her cleaned and dressed. It was May and hot out so Tiff put Brandy out a pink little dress and some black flip flops. I put oil in her curly hair and her pink white gold earrings that Kimmora and Kevin brought her on her 1st birthday. Brandy was turning two on July 4th and I couldn't wait.

Her birthday would be in Miami and me and Tiff wanted to have a big celebration. I knew my brothers and their wives would come to Miami to celebrate with us. Shit, me and my bros had illegal business in Miami. That was like our second home, so I knew I wouldn't miss my bros too much and Tiff would see the girls a lot too. After I got Brandy dressed I turned her TV on to My Little Pony cartoon. My squeak loved that annoying ass cartoon. I kissed her on her cheeks and let her play with her toys.

Walking to our bedroom Tiff was in the bathroom putting her hair in a high bun. I knew she was about to get in the shower. I of course was going to join her. I stripped out my clothes and walked in the bathroom with my dick swinging. Tiff looked at me through the mirror, actually she was looking at my dick, and she bit her lip. I smirked and turned the shower on. If I had to bet all my millions, I would bet that she was wet as fuck and I was going to be able to get a quick one in while we showered. As we stepped in Tiff had that look in her eye and without saying shit. I picked her sexy ass up and kissed her. Told y'all! Ha!

Tiff

As I drove my orange Land Rover Discovery I looked in my rear-view mirror at my baby girl. She was eating her little bag of bananas I cut up for her. My baby was so damn pretty and chocolate. She looked just like her daddy which pissed me off. I figured I spent seventeen hours in labor with her. I stretched my pussy hole in a way that is unimaginable, ya damn right she should look like me. But, she was a spitting image of my fine ass husband except my skin tone and eye shape. This was still my mini me and I couldn't be more blessed to have her.

We were on our way to Kylee's house to hang with her and my other sisters. I was going to drop Brandy over my parents' house and go hang. But we leave for Miami in two days and the girls would kill me if they couldn't see Brandy before we left. As Brandon told y'all earlier, I was so nervous about this Miami move. Part of it was me just being nervous about starting over in a new place. Far from family, friends and familiar surroundings. The other part is Brandon and his past in Miami. Y'all heard what he did and how her hurt me. If he was to ever do that again may God be with that man. I think I feared for him more than me being heartbroken.

After talking to my mama, the other day and her telling me to have faith in God and in my husband, I felt a little better. I got into some prayer and I trust in God more than I trust in some stupid fear. The way I was set up and my family were, I knew that if things ever were to get bad between me and Brandon to the point where he cheated. I would leave and be ok with being a single parent. Of course, I would be hurt and go through that break up faze. But I know I would have done all I could and was a good wife to that man. So, for now all my fear was gone. Now, I was more anxious. I was ready to get the moving, packing and unpacking over with.

Me and Brandon found a gorgeous five-bedroom home in South West Miami. I was so excited to furnish it and fix my baby girl's room up. I didn't want to shock her too much with all the change. So, I made sure to do an exact replica of her room that she had here in New Orleans. We decided to keep our home here. The girls or the guys would stop by to check on it and our maid would keep it clean. Because Louisiana would always be home, we knew keeping the house was a smart move. I was excited to start my job at the gym. Karlos had opened up his second location in Miami.

He asked me if I would run it since I was the workout queen. Yoga and pilates were my specialty. My mother used to be in bodybuilding competitions when I was little. My father was as well except he was a heavy weight. And he was fit from being in the Army. That's how they met, at a competition and by the time a winner was chosen my dad was fuckin' my mama in the locker room. I'm being a bit graphic, my mother cleaned up the version for me when I was little but being an adult now. I knew exactly what she meant. Anyways, they have been together ever since. My mama is older than my dad by nine years. She was twenty-eight when she met my dad and he was nineteen. Yup. My mama was a fucking cougar!

My mama looked like Angela Basset when she played Tina Turner in the movie What's Love Got to Do with It." In fact, when I was little I used to think that was my mama getting beat up on. I used to cry, and she would have to calm me down. Tilly Johnson was beautiful with brown skin and she stood at 5'6. She has long black hair and a body that a woman who is almost in her sixties would kill to have. Her and my dad were vegans and still worked out and took care of themselves. My dad, Theo Johnson is 6'5 and weights around 300lbs. I forget but either way it was all muscle. He was caramel skin tone with a bald head and a goatee.

Him and my mama are a beautiful couple and they are the number one thing I will miss about leaving Louisiana. I'm an only child and me and my parents are very close. I'm the true daddy's girl and mama's baby. I have never lived more than an hour away from them and at least every other day I see them. Me and my mama had a good relationship and she was my best friend. Her only down fall was how critical she is about weight. Being fat or juicy was never an option with my mama. The weight I picked up after my pregnancy, she hated it. But, I loved it and so did Brandon. I never really had a lot of female friends growing up. I was one of the few who had both parents in the home. I was spoiled rotten and it made kids not like me.

Tilly and Theo never raised me to be stuck up or to think I was better than anyone. I actually used to try to buy friends with my toys and big house. But, no matter what I did I could not make any friends. So, I spent a lot of time alone or with my parents. My dad's family was all in Jamaica and I never saw them or knew them. My mama's parents died when I was little, and she was an only child. When I met Brandon, and got close to him and his brothers, that was the closest I have ever had to having siblings. When I tell y'all those are my big brother's and they played the part to the T! That's why I was happy as hell when they met my girls and they locked their wild asses down.

Throughout middle and high school, I stayed in shape. Now, don't get me wrong I ate candy and all other sweets that kids loved. But I always enjoyed working out with my mama and going to the gym with her. Over the years, I had jobs at gyms and dance classes. I went to college and graduated with a bachelors in Physical Education. That's why I jumped at the opportunity to run Karlos' gym. My big brother let me decorate it and have the layout anyway I wanted. I love my brothers!

Pulling up to Kylee's house I saw all my sister's cars there. I smiled big as hell because I loved these girls so much. I went to college with Kimmora and me and her hit it off instantly. I invited her and her sisters to The Royal's party, but I had never met her sisters before. When I did, we clicked like me and Kimmora and we all are joined at the hip. Our guys loved our relationship but got annoyed by it too. We stuck together and when one of our guys messed up we were all ready to fight. We annoyed them, but they love the fuck out of us. I grabbed Brandy out her car seat and picked her now sleep self-up. I don't know why I didn't grab her diaper bag first. Now I had to carry her little chunky butt to the other side of my truck and grab her bag.

"Why the hell you ain't call in the house so I could come out and help you?" I rolled my eyes and smiled when I heard my big brother's deep ass voice scare the neighbor's dog.

"I don't know smart ass." I laughed as he took Brandy out my arms and grabbed her bag.

"As long as my brother not here then you know I got you. I'm about to lay my niece down in her room. They loud asses in my man cave fuckin' it up." Karlos told me as we walked in him and Kylee's house. I laughed at his comment.

"What'chu mean fuckin' it up?" What are they in there doing?" I grabbed Brandy's diaper bag off Karlos arm, so I could put her water and juice in the ice box.

"My man cave smells like niggas, weed and cologne. Now y'all in there makin' it smell like perfume, gossip and pussy." I fell out laughing at his silly ass!

"Karlos I can't with you. Your supposed to be at

Kaylin house anyways with the guys." I was still laughing as I closed the ice box. Putting Brandy's bag on the bar stool in the kitchen. Karlos was still holding her and she was knocked out.

"I'm about to dip out now after I lay my niece down." He bent down so I could kiss my baby on the cheek. We all had a room for each other's kids at our homes. We were moving to Miami and I still did a room for my nieces and nephews.

While Karlos went upstairs to lay Brandy down I went down the hall to his man cave. I smiled when I heard my sisters loud as hell and Sza's album playing. When I walked in the room the girls were sitting in the movie style recliners. Kimmora must have made mimosa's because they all had an orange drink in their hands. On the bar I saw some wine and orange juice.

"Sis!" Kylee jumped up and hugged me. The rest of them smiled big and hugged me too.

"Hey y'all! Kylee, yo crazy ass husband took Brandy from me and laid her down so stop mugging me." I rolled my eyes jokingly at her. Kimmora passed me a drink. I noticed Kelly was drinking some slush drink.

"Sis what are you drinking?" I asked taking a seat next to her.

"Girl, Kaylin threatened me about drinking alcohol because I'm still breastfeeding the twins. I told him I already pumped some milk for them, but he wasn't tyrna hear it." She rolled her eyes and we laughed. Kelly gave birth to Kennedy and Kenny two months ago. They were beautiful with a head full of hair and those famous light grey eyes. I was so happy for her and Kaylin and they were soaking up this parenthood thing.

"So, y'all made me bring Brandy but all my babies are gone?" I was mad at them because I wanted to see them before we left.

"Hush up, we are all coming over you and Brandon's house the day before y'all leave." Keira said smiling.

"And I wanted to bring the twins, but Kaylin claims they are only two-months and they're not ready for the world yet." Kelly said shaking her head and laughing. Kaylin was so overprotective of the twins. It was so cute but annoying as hell to Kelly.

Karlos walked in the room and told Kylee to come here. After a couple of minutes she came back smiling hard as fuck and biting her lip. We all laughed and shook our heads at her. Now, me and Brandon have a love that runs deep. But Karlos and Kylee's love sucked you in and it wasn't even yo' relationship. It was such a beautiful thing but was nothing to play with or try to come between.

"So, are you ok now as far as your feeling towards moving to Miami?" Kelly asked while Kylee turned the music down. It was safe to talk now that Karlos was gone.

"I am now. I had a talk with Brandon but what really helped me feel better was getting into some prayer. I was just scared with Brandon being back in the place that he cheated on me. But, a man is going to do what he wants no matter the location. I just have to trust in God and know that he has me." I smiled at them meaning every word I just said.

"I understand where you're coming from Tiff. I still get a certain feeling when we go to the guys' club. Hell, I even thought about Karlos giving that club up if I was going to take him back when he cheated on me. But, like you I realized all that forcing a man to do shit is not going to stop him from fucking up. I had to heal and really see if I can put trust in him again. Either way just like y'all had me with that decision. You know we got you the same way." Kylee said making me smile big and tear up. I got up and hugged her, and the rest of the girls joined in.

"Besides, if Brandon acts stupid we will turn Miami

the fuck out. Remember Kimmora cussed Kaylin out for filth! And God be a fence on how she lit into Karlos." Keira laughed, and we cracked up.

"I don't give a damn! Y'all know I don't play about my sisters. But all jokes aside, Tiff you know we got you. Go on down to Miami and enjoy life just like you do here. Y'all being down there will give us a reason to visit Miami a lot." Kimmora said as she raised her glass and we toasted to myself, Brandon and Brandy's new beginning. We chilled, drunk mimosas and listened to music for the rest of the evening. I was going to miss doing this anytime I wanted. Even though I knew we still would be close and see each other. The distance would just take some adjustment. We were all ten-minutes from each other and now I am about to be a two-hour flight away or an almost fifteen-hour drive. I am going to miss seeing my sisters everyday but new beginnings is always nice. Bring it on Miami!

Blair

(In Miami)

"WHERE THE FUCK WERE YOU BLAIR? AND IF YOU LIE AGAIN I'M TELLING YOU WE GONE HAVE A PROBLEM!" Raheem stood over me looking at me with anger all in his eyes.

"Raheem baby, I am not lying to you. I was at work with Sarah. I would have been off early, but someone called off. Melissa told me that I had to stay an extra hour." I took my chances and walked closer to him. His eyes stayed glued to me as I approached his 6'0 slim body. I reached my hand up to caress the side of his face while still looking in his eyes.

"I am not cheating on you booskie. I'm sorry that I didn't call you I didn't think------" My words were cut off when Raheem put his hand around my neck and walked me backwards until my back was pressed against the wall.

"See, that's your fucking problem. You don't fuckin' THINK! You know you check in with me every hour on the hour. Why the fuck do you like seeing me like this? You think I like hurting my precious angel face, huh?" I shook my head no. Raheem squeezed harder around my neck. Then he leaned closer to my body and licked all over my face covering my entire face with his wet tongue.

"Naw, you don't taste like another nigga so you might be telling the truth. The next time you don't call me like you're supposed to shit is going to get really bad for you Blair." He slammed my head against the wall and walked away." I watched him go downstairs and once I knew he was in the basement. I slid down the wall and cried.

I know your probably thinking why am I with someone like him? But me and Raheem's relationship was not always like this. I met him two years ago. He was still sexy physically like he is now and he sure as hell didn't show the side of him that you just witnessed. As a matter of fact, everything is still the same. We still go on dates, trips, shopping sprees and the sex is so damn good the shit is ridiculous. But Raheem couldn't keep his dick in his pants. He got caught slippin' last year. A bitch approached me and told me she was pregnant by him.

Now, Raheem is hot out here in Miami as an up and coming rapper. So, it was common for bitches to want what's mine. I blew her off as a groupie bitch until she showed me photos and text messages. I almost died right there in front of her. When I approached Raheem about the situation he told me he would handle it. No bullshit, those were his exact words to me before he walked out the house we share. The next day he came up to my job with the bitch and had her give me abortion papers. I could not believe the shit that was before my eyes.

I held it together until I got off work. My mind was set on leaving his crazy ass when I got to our house. I had packed my shit and was headed out the door when Raheem came home and caught me. He started crying and begging me to stay. You never would think a nigga as hard and rough as Raheem would be shedding tears over a woman leaving him. Bitches lined up at his feet for him and here he was begging me. The nigga had tears and snot running all down his face. I wasn't moved one fuckin' bit. I still headed to the door and that's when he pulled me by my hair. He didn't hit me, but he slammed me against the wall so hard he bruised my back all up.

Raheem started telling me he would kill me if I leave him and he would kill my mama and best friend. My mama really made me no mind, but my best friend Sarah was my heart. He laid some good dick and head on me and fucked me so hard that even a hot bath didn't help. I tried to leave a few times after that but he always either found me or caught me before I would make it out the door. It was all the same thing, he would never hit me just rough me up until the last time I tried. He locked me in the basement for a month. He kept me fed and clean, but I didn't see nothing but the basement for thirty fucking days. I lost my good ass job I had at this insurance office.

The only way he would let me out was if I promised to never leave and I followed his rules. I agreed just so I could leave. When he let me go Raheem started acting possessive over me out of fear that I would leave. Things between us went back to normal and because I lost my job because of him he offered to pay my tuition for community college and he brought me a 2017 Buick Regal which I loved. Besides rapping Raheem stole expensive cars and resold them at a higher price. I had always wanted my college degree to prove to my ain't shit of a mother that I was better than what she thought I was. So, I stayed with Raheem and made it work.

I would be lying if I said I didn't love him. Hell, he was fine, paid, had good dick and tongue game. He listened to me when I would talk his ear off about my dreams, he cuddled and can cook his ass off. He just had one small problem with control but nobody's perfect. I got myself together and went to the bathroom to take a shower. I pulled my maxi dress over my head and put my hair in a bun. I looked in the mirror at my bruised neck and rubbed my fingers across it. It didn't hurt but you could see Raheem's nail prints. I looked at my reflection and knew that as much as I loved Raheem, I had to get out this mess of a relationship.

I was a beautiful girl and the one thing I had to thank my raggedy ass parents for were my good looks and body. I stood at 5'7 with smooth brown skin and a face sculpted by angles, or so that's what Raheem says. I had full lips, brown eyes and a body bitches hated on, and niggas loved to love on. My ass was nice as fuck and it matched my hips and flat stomach perfectly. I was told I look like the bitch T.I. left Tiny's ass for. I don't know about all that, I personally thought I looked better but whatever. I stepped in the hot shower and let the water wet my entire body up including my hair. I had the best of the best hair sewed in, so I was good.

Closing my eyes, I thought back to why my life had taken this nasty ass turn. All I wanted was love, success and happiness. I thought I had it, but I guess God said 'Got that ass' to me. My insurance job that paid so well and offered health insurance was long gone. Now I was working at Wendy's flipping burgers and dealing with greasy ass food all day. I was assistant manager but it still didn't pay like my last job. And I had to hide my body under that nasty ass uniform. Raheem said I didn't have to work but I lied and told him that my financial aid required me to have a job. His stupid uneducated ass didn't know shit about that, so he believed me. There was no way I was about to depend on him.

As the water rand down my body I heard the shower curtain slide across the pole. I felt Raheem step in. I didn't even acknowledge him but of course, he gently grabbed my arm and turned me around. He lifted my chin so that I could look at him. As soon as I did my pussy pushed me to the left and took over. She got so wet and I felt my clit swell up at the sight if Raheem chocolate ass. His waves were still deep even with water on them. His six pack was looking more plumped up then normal, so I know he must have been working out. His face was perfect with all white teeth, a thin goatee and mustache that brought his pink lips out more. He looked like Lance Gross fine ass. Swear Raheem could be his twin!

"I love you angel face, so fucking much. I cannot

ever lose you that's why we have rules. I walked around with the panties you wore yesterday in my pocket all day. That's how much I missed you angel face. I felt like I was about to die when an hour passed and I didn't hear from you." As he spoke he lifted me up and set me on the rack that held our shower gels and shampoos.

"All these thoughts went through my head of never seeing you again." His big hands were moving all over my body. His eyes followed where his hands touched. I looked at him with my eyes filled with lust. My pussy was drenched, and it wasn't the water doing it.

"How could I live without seeing my sweet angel face ever again? Do you understand how that would fuck me up?" He slid two of his big fingers in my pussy.

As soon as he did that my pussy muscles latched on to his fingers making him smirk at me. Raheem was finger fucking me so good. His deep voice against my ear wrapped around my body like silk. I was about to cum when he slid his fingers out and dropped to his knees. He opened my lips all the way so my clit was exposed. He attacked that first making me shudder. Raheem's tongue was so thick, and he knew how to add the right pressure. He knew when to suck, pull, lick and kiss my clit. He never used his fingers when he ate my pussy because he never had to. I felt like I was about to explode!

"Oh my God Raheem babeeee! Ugh!" I know my legs were choking him, but he never complained. When I came he licked it all up and he kissed his way up my body. When he stood back up he shoved his hard 9-inch black dick in me. I stopped breathing for a second the shit felt so good.

"Eyes on me angel face." He demanded while he fucked me hard. His hand went around my neck tight almost choking me. I looked at him and he had tears coming down his face while he bit his bottom lip.

"I don't want to kill you, but you will leave me with

no choice if you leave me. If I can't find you then your mama and best friend will be done for. All this shit can be avoided if you just follow my rules. Ugh fuck angel face you got some good pussy!" I leaned my head back and closed my eyes. Raheem's dick felt like hitting the mega million over and over!

"Raheem babe I'm never leaving you I swear!" His dick had me saying shit I didn't mean but charge it to the good dick and not my mouth. He pulled my head up by my neck and kissed me. Raheem kisses always left me wanting him more. He fucked me so good and hard I didn't even pay attention to the shower getting cold. How could someone so perfect have such flaws?

*

The next day

"Angel face where the fuck are you going?" Raheem asked as he followed me downstairs. I rolled my eyes because he followed me all through the house all day every day like a damn puppy.

"Raheem I'm going to see my mama. It's Friday remember, I'm going to pay her rent and bring her some groceries." He stood there looking pissed off. Today was hot as fuck in Miami so I had on jean shorts and an orange tank top. I kept it simple with some flip flops and my Brazilian sew-in in a ponytail. Raheem looked good as hell with some basketball shorts on and a white muscle beater. If he wasn't so annoying I would have stayed under him all day.

"Angel face I don't know why the fuck you keep paying her fucking rent. Fuck yo' mama and stay with yo' man." He raised his voice a little. I knew how to fix this shit.

I walked up to him with my eyes still connecting with his. I dropped to my knees and pulled his basketball shorts down. His dick sprung out and was in my face. I licked my lips and took him all in my mouth. Raheem's dick grew a few more inches in my throat. He took the back of my head and pushed me further into him. I didn't gag because I was that bitch! Raheem was moaning, and I heard his toes crack in his slide-ins. I kept sucking and sucking until I was swallowing his nut. I wiped the corners of his mouth and pulled his shorts up. I stood up nice and slow. I was so turned on, so I knew when I got back I was throwing this pussy on him.

"I'll be back babe, I promise." I was about to walk away before he grabbed my arm with all his strength. I caught my breath in my throat and my heart started beating fast. I didn't want to show any signs of fear because then I would never be able to leave.

"Raheem babe, let me go. I promise I'm coming back to you." I kept looking at him as his grip got tighter. I was slowly nodding my head yes as he loosened up his grip and I was able to slide my arm out his grip.

"I love you and I'll be back." I walked backwards because the last time I turned my back to him he grabbed my hair.

Once I was out the door I hit the alarm to my car and got in. I took a deep breath and looked down at my arm. Thank God, he didn't bruise it. I turned my key and cut some music on. Driving to my mother's apartment I had my air conditioner blowing in my face. I seriously dreaded these visits with my mother. But I knew if her rent wasn't paid then she would be on the streets and I couldn't have that. Not because I loved her but because her crack head ass would be trying to live with me.

All my life my mom had been on drugs. Her and my dad used to send me to get the drugs from the local drug dealers when we lived back home in Ohio. That's where I was born and raised, in Cleveland, Ohio. I was an only child up until I was ten years old. My mother got pregnant by her drug dealer and she gave birth at our house in the bathroom. I was only ten years old helping my dad deliver a baby. When she pushed the baby out it died the next day. My parents didn't even care or notice because they were so high. I had to dispose of the baby in a dumpster after I kissed my little brother and cried for him.

The only thing my parents were good at was making sure I stayed in designer clothes and we stayed in a nice house. They were crack heads who could afford their habit because my dad had a good job. He was a construction worker and he made a lot of money because he was good at what he did and he worked all year long. One day he went to work high out his mind and his boss sent him home for good. After that my dad got so depressed and we slowly lost everything. Our house, cars, clothes and I lost the luxury of going to a good private school. We moved in with my dad's brother. I guess my dad couldn't take the pressure because when I was fifteen he put a rifle to his head.

Now, even though my dad was around me every day. He still was a shitty father and I hated him to the core. He touched on me from the time I was little until the time he died. My mother knew too because she walked in on us one day. I cried and ran to my mother because I thought she was going to protect me. I thought the nightmare was over and me and her would leave his sick ass and live happily ever after. Well I was wrong, my mother slapped me so hard across my face. She told me how dare I seduce my own father.

I was only eight years old then and I wanted to die. I couldn't believe my mother would think I would do anything like that to my dad. I was not familiar with sex or anything of that nature until my sick ass father opened that door. After that day I shut down and didn't talk to my parents. They thought I was retarded but never tried to do anything about it. My dad told me if I got to school and told anyone I would have to leave my room and all my toys. So, I never opened my mouth and my mother turned the other cheek. It wasn't until I was thirteen when he started actually having sex with me.

I had lost my virginity to my own father. I cried and cried every day after that to the point where I wanted to run away. But I had nowhere to go and we had no other family. I had no friends because I stopped talking and the kids called me weird and slow. I just kept to myself. When I turned fourteen I met a friend in school named Sarah Patterson. She was so nice and for some reason I took to her to the point where I started talking again. We were stuck together like glue. One day I spent the night at her house and I told her about my dad. She panicked and told her parents and within the next few days I was living with them. I was so happy because I felt like I had a real family.

Sarah's parents were normal. They had a dog, rules that were easy to follow and we used to have game night. Sarah was white and she had the typical 'Full House' family. I used to feel like I was in an afternoon sitcom when I lived with them and I soaked it up. My parents begged me to come back home especially my mom. She claimed my dad was a mess since I was gone. But I knew better than that and I stayed with Sarah and her family. On my 15th birthday my dad blew his brains out and my mom blamed me every fucking day. She stayed on drugs and went further downhill. I was told from her that I never would amount to shit because I let my own father die of a broken heart. When me and Sarah turned eighteen we moved to Miami with her auntie. She let us stay with her until we got on our feet and got our own place.

One-day last year I got a phone call from some guy at a rehab center in Ohio. He told me my mother was sick and needed me. I had a soft spot for my mama and I could not understand why. Anyways, I flew to Ohio to see her. I was told by her doctors that she was dying, and the drugs have worn her body down. I felt bad, so I flew her back to Miami with me and set her up in a senior citizen apartment. The rent was three-hundred a month and I agreed to pay it. I thought she was dying soon but here we are. A whole year later and she is still kicking. Calling me names and telling me how much she hates me.

I could easily leave her the money and have her pay her rent and buy her own groceries. But hell no, I knew better than that. I paid he neighbor downstairs from her a hundred dollars month to check in on her and make sure she was fine, Ester was a nice woman and she had no problem with helping out.

I parked my car into my mother's apartment complex. Before I got out I took a selfie of myself and sent it to Raheem letting him know I was at my mom's. He responded with 'Hurry back angel face' with the angry emojis. I put the kissing emoji and got out the car. Walking up to the leasing office some old farts were looking at me like I was some denture cream. I rolled my eyes and walked in the office. The smell of boiled cabbage and icy hot hit my nose.

"Hey Chuck! It's that time of the month again!" I yelled making him walk to the front. He was an old Hispanic man who was about 300lbs and stood about 5'5. His wife was never too far behind him. Veronica was around my age with a fat ass and small waist. She was Hispanic as well with long black hair. In case you're wondering Chuck owns two nice apartment buildings including this one and on upscale one in the middle of Miami attraction. He owns four homes and three Five Guys restaurants in Florida. So that should explain Veronica!

"Black beauty, hello my love. Always on time!" I smiled and laughed every time he called me that. Chuck swore up and down that I was going to be his wife. He even said the shit in front of Veronica.

"You know it boo. Here ya go." I smiled at him and handed him my mama's rent. Veronica walked up front with a smug expression. She didn't like me because Chuck made it known he wanted me.

"Blair, how are you today mami? I see you're gaining weight all in the wrong places." She said with her thick accent sitting on Chuck's lap. He turned his nose up at her as he wrote my receipt out. I laughed at her hating ass because she knew damn well I was the shit and if I wanted to, I could have her meal ticket.

"I'm doing well boo. And as far as the weight I wouldn't worry about that. I know someone who likes it." I looked at Chuck as he gave me my receipt and I winked at him making him smile and sweat. Veronica smacked her lips and as I walked out I heard her yell at him in Spanish. I laughed and kept laughing as I headed to my mother's apartment.

When I walked in my mama's apartment I knew Ester must have come today. I could smell apple cinnamon in the air. Ester always baked my mother an apple pie when she checked on her. I brought my mother furniture when she first came down here. She hated it and claimed brown and cream were ugly colors. I picked them because that was the color of our living room when I was little. My mother didn't hate it, she just hated it because I picked it out. She claimed her bedroom set was cheap and her mattress was hard. I paid three-thousand for her bedroom set and fifteen-hundred for her king size mattress. She was just being a bitch like always.

"What the fuck is yo' stank ass doing here?" She looked at me when I walked in her bedroom. My mother was a beautiful woman, but her insides were all fucked up and twisted. She was 5'6 with chocolate skin, shoulder length hair and because she did drugs for so many years, her body looked worn out and tired.

"Hi to you too mama. I just paid your rent. I was coming to see if you needed any groceries?" I stood in the door and looked at her. I saw tissues and my trifling ass dad's pictures all over her bed, so I knew she was having one of her days.

"Why the hell you announcing that shit? You're supposed to take care of me, I gave you fucking life. And what thanks do I get?" I rolled my eyes because I knew what was coming next.

"You killed the love of my life for your own selfish reasons." Her voice started breaking and tears fell from her eyes.

"Oh, yea right mama, I'm the one who put the rifle in his hand." I said as I turned my nose up and got annoyed.

"You might as well! He died from a broken heart that his own daughter gave him!" She started yelling and crying bad.

"I didn't come here for this shit. I came to see if you needed anything from the store." I stated matter of factly.

"GET THE FUCK OUT! I DON'T NEED SHIT FROM YOU!" When she started screaming I knew it was time to go. She got herself all worked up and started coughing bad as hell. I continued out the door.

"I HATE YOU BLAIR! WHY COULDN'T YOU HAVE DIED AND NOT HIM!" That was the last thing I heard as I closed her door. I laughed and shook my head.

Anybody else would have broken down hearing their mother shout that. But I was so used to her hateful words and actions. The only thing that would make me break down is if she showed me some love. I unlocked my car and got in. Taking my phone out I texted Sarah and told her to take my shift tomorrow morning and I'd take her night shift. She agreed, and I smiled. I didn't feel like getting up in the morning and dealing with Wendy's. I texted Raheem and told him I was on my way home. He responded with a picture of his hard dick. I bit my lip and put my phone down and started my care up. I put my gear in drive and headed home. Some good dick will ease my mind after dealing with my damn mama.

Brandon

I stood looking at the grave sight of Kaine and Staci Royal. I put flowers on mama Staci's grave and I put a Gurkha Black Dragon cigar on Kaine's grave. He loved those things and smoked them only on holiday's. After I paid respect to the best people to ever come into my life after Tiff and my daughter. I went to the grave and that was hard for me to go to every time her birthday came. I felt my palms get warm and my stomach hurt. I walked slowly, and it felt like I was walking the green mile.

"You got this babe. I'm right here with you." My wife's sweet voice interrupted my thoughts. Her voice took away my fear. I nodded my head and stepped in front of the grave site. Evelyn Ann Williams was written on the tomb stone with a beautiful picture of her face on it. I missed this woman so much and not a day went by when I didn't think about her. I owed her my life and it was because of her I had life. I kneeled down and just looked at her picture for a second.

"Hey old lady. I know it's been a minute since I visited you, but you know you still my favorite girl. I couldn't leave Louisiana without seeing you and telling you the news. Me and Tiff decided to move to Miami. We got new chapters beginning and unfortunately, it's not in Louisiana. I already can hear your voice. "Brandon, go see the world chile and take that pretty brown skin girl with you. You know I love her pretty white teeth." I mocked what she used to tell me all the time. Me and Tiff laughed.

"Well I'm taking your advice and starting a new journey with my family. Brandy is doing so good. She is getting so big and she is beautiful just like her mama. I'm gone have to kill niggas over her I can see it now. I miss you so much old lady and I promise to come back March 2nd to see you. I love you so much grandma and I will do my best to keep making you proud of me." I kissed my hand and touched her gave. I had tears coming from my eyes but that was always anytime I even talked about my grandma.

I looked at her picture again and her pretty brown eyes and dark skin made her snow white long hair stand out. I kissed my hand again but this time I touched her picture. Standing up I felt Tiff's soft hand grab mine. I felt calm but still sadness in my heart for my grandma. The tears were coming down. Tiff turned and hugged me, and I broke down. I missed my grandma so much and hated that she left me so soon. I wanted to take her with me around the world. I wanted her to be at my wedding and see my first child come into this world. I felt cheated out of my time with her.

My grandma stepped in and took me when I was a few months old. My mama was a singer and wanted life on the road more than her own son. Nobody knows who my father is because it was just a one-night fling between him and my mama. For as long as I could remember it has been me and my grandma. Every phase in my life from my first words, first tooth I lost, to my first step. My grandma has been right there. I remember a woman coming to see me sometimes. She was beautiful and always had a different man with her. She would pick me up, kiss me and leave my grandma some money. One day when I was seven years old, my grandma told me that woman who used to visit me was my mama. She told me she was killed in a shooting and would not be coming to visit me anymore.

I didn't cry like I should have. Hell, I didn't feel shit because as far as I was concerned my grandma was my mama. I felt bad for not caring but it is what it is. The one horrible memory I had with my grandma was her boyfriend Ray. That nigga was the devil and I hated him. He used to beat my grandma's ass. Every time he would come in drunk my grandma would put me in the closet and tell me not to come out until she got me. I used to hear him screaming at her and slapping her around. I hated every moment of that shit and never understood why my grandma didn't kill that nigga. Ray kept guns in the house and he taught me at the age of six how to hold a gun and shoot it. My grandma knew how to shoot too because she would take me hunting with them and her aim was better than Ray's.

I asked her all the time why she loved him. She told me something's are understood between and man and a woman that no one else understood. I knew she was right because I didn't understand what the hell she had just said. My grandma hugged me and told me she would be ok and so would I. We didn't have much, my grandma sold dinners and her sorry ass nigga worked at a dry cleaner. One of my grandma's customers who loved her cooking was a woman named Staci Royal. She used to come over all the time with her sons and we would play together.

You could tell the way they dressed that they were from money. But they never treated me any different. My grandma would teach their mama how to cook her famous meals. I believe Staci just enjoyed my grandma's company. My grandma had an energy about her that made you want to be around her. Anyways, when Staci would come over with her sons we would go outside and play. One day some older kids came and fucked with us. They knew me and knew I didn't have shit. But they looked at Kevin, Kalvin and Kaylin and saw money.

Theses niggas had to be about fourteen and we were only seven and eight. I knew we were about to get beat up, but I was still ready to hold my own. I looked at Kevin, Kalvin and Kaylin and they were ready too. Some bum across the street saw what was about to happen and he yelled some shit that made those niggas take off and run like the road runner.

"Aye, you niggas better leave them alone! Those are Kaine Royal's boys.!" The bum yelled from across the street. The bullies looked at us and took off down the street.

I was shocked as fuck and that's when Kevin told me about their pops. He also told me they had an older brother who was always with their pops. I was impressed and knew I wanted to be down with them. My grandma and Staci saw how good we got along. So, Staci suggested I go to the same school as her sons. My grandma turned her down because she had no way of getting me to school every morning and she damn sure couldn't afford the tuition. The private school was far as hell from where we stayed. Staci told her to not worry about all of that. From that day on I was getting picked up every morning and driven to school. I was in the same class as Kevin and Kalvin. Kaylin was a year younger than us, so he was in a different class.

I was coming out of class one day with Kevin and Kalvin. I saw some tall nigga with a lot of hair getting this fine ass girl's number. Our school went from Kindergarten through the eighth grade. Every nigga with a dick knew about Lana's fine ass. She was in the eighth grade and built better than most of the teachers. When she gave her number to the yellow nigga he hit her on the ass and walked off. Walking towards us I'm thinking we are about to fight because he is about to fuck with us. He dapped Kevin and Kalvin up and looked at me like he wanted to hang my ass by the neck.

"Who the fuck are you and why you around my brothers?" I looked at his tall ass and even though he could whoop my ass. I still wasn't about to show no fear.

"I'm Brandon and I'm around them because these

my friends. Who the fuck are you?" I asked him with the same tone he had. This tall nigga looked at me and smiled. But I swear that shit made my little ass shake. His smile was nothing of a normal person and his eyes looked like he needed to be locked up away from anything humane. Kalvin stepped in front of us and held his hand on the tall nigga's chest.

"Karlos, this is our friend Brandon. Remember I told you some big niggas was about to jump us. Well, Brandon was right there ready to fight with us." When Kalvin said that Karlos calmed down and he looked at me with a friendlier expression.

"My fault bro. I don't fuck around about my brothers. But if you was down for them then I'm down for you." He balled his fist out and held it out. I looked at him and dapped him up.

"How did you get Lana to give you her number. I know you not in eighth grade because your locker is where ours is at." I asked because I was intrigued by his skills to pull an older girl. Karlos laughed as we walked to the lunch room.

"Man, Lana a nasty hoe and she been wanting me for a while. I wouldn't stick my dick in her, but I would stick it in her mouth. If you want. I'll get her to hook you up too. Just a thank you for looking out for my brothers." I tried to keep my cool on his offer. I was dancing on the inside because I had never been with a girl. I was starting to feel my body go through these changes whenever I was around them. I took Karlos up on his offer and just like he said within two days Lana was sucking my dick. From then on out those Royal niggas became my brothers.

Months went by and shit was good. I was loving my new school and me and my bros were getting along smooth as hell. Hanging with them made the girls flock and I was loving it. Karlos ass was the leader and he was crazy as hell. He was smart as fuck, hell all of us were, but he was so fucking mean. He was even mean to all the girls no matter how fine they were. Shit was good except my home life. Ray was getting more and more mean and physical with my grandma. One day I came home from school and him and my grandma were arguing. He was mad because he wanted some money and my grandma wouldn't give it to him.

She was telling him that I needed the money for my football uniform. He was getting madder and madder. When he hit her, and knocked her into the kitchen table I snapped. I ran to my grandma's room and pulled her shot gun from under her bed. I creeped back in the dining room and this sick nigga was standing over my grandma peeing on her. Tears fell from my face and I was breathing hard. I cocked the shot gun back and pointed it at him. He picked his head up turning around to face me. Putting his dick up he smiled and looked at the gun.

"Lil nigga you better be prepared to use that." Before I knew it, I had shot a hole through his stomach. He dropped to his knees and fell forward. My grandma sat up slowly with her face messed up. She looked at him and then looked at me. I dropped the gun and wiped my face. My grandma crawled to me until she was on her knees and in my face. She cried and hugged me making me cry hard. I told her I was sorry, and she said,

"No, I'm sorry Brandon. I should have did what you did a long time ago. I don't want you to feel scared or anything. Grandma will handle this." She got up and went to the bathroom. When I heard her in the shower I picked up our house phone and called Kevin to tell him what happened. About an hour passed and my grandma covered up Ray's body with a sheet. Her face was fucked up. She had a swollen bottom lip and her left eye was shut closed and swollen as well. I cried just looking at her.

"Brandon, I am going to call the police and tell them

I shot Ray because he was beating me. I want you to agree with me and when the police handcuff me I want you to cooperate with them and do as they say." My grandma instructed me. Before I could say anything, a knock came to the door. My grandma jumped with fear it was a neighbor.

She looked out the peep hole and looked at me. When she opened the door it was Staci, my bros and some yellow muscle nigga. He looked just like my bros so I figured it was their pops. Staci cried when she saw my grandma's face and she hugged her. They all walked in and closed the door.

"Karlos, take your brothers and Brandon to the back." Their pops said and we followed Karlos to my room. I was still in shock and my tears kept coming down. I didn't even try to front when my bros came. Hell, my grandma was going to jail and who knew what was going to happen to me.

"Brandon, stop crying bro. My pops and mama got this and will make all this go away. You dropped your first body, You a Royal now." Karlos said to me with a smirk. I looked at him and at the rest of my bros. They smirked too and nodded their heads. Karlos held his fist out. I dabbed him up and the rest of my brothers dabbed me up as well.

"We ain't have to drop nobody yet, only Karlos. He liked the shit so we know how he feels. What about you though, was it scary?" Kaylin asked me.

"I mean, the nigga was hurting my grandma. So, all I thought about was making him stop so no. it wasn't scary. The shit felt good." I said as I wiped my face. They nodded and Karlos crazy ass smiled and gave me a low five.

I guess Karlos was right because a few hours later we left my grandma's house and never came back. I don't know what happened to Ray's body, but it was gone and the house was spotless. Me and my grandma went to live with Staci and Kaine. I lived there all through elementary, and middle school. And up until my junior year of high school. By then I had moved into my own place, but Staci wanted my grandma to stay with her. I thought it was weird at first, but I figured if that's what my grandma wanted then I was cool with it.

Junior year I had my own apartment and own car. I didn't punch nobody's clock either. I worked with my bros and their pops and uncles (them bitch ass niggas). By the time I was sixteen, I knew all there was to know about the game. I even got my hands dirty with Karlos' ass. I don't think I enjoyed it as much as him, but I still was down. We used my spot to smash bitches because Mama Staci didn't play about bringing hoes in her house.

None of us had a steady girlfriend because who wanted to be locked down with one bitch. Too much pussy out here and we wanted to sample it all. Shit changed for me when I met Tiff's fine ass. But that's another story for another chapter. Shit was back smooth until one day I came home from school. Staci said her, and my grandma wanted to talk to me. They sat me down and told me my grandma was sick with breast cancer. I was ready to dish out whatever money it took to get her better. Mama Staci told me they had been trying different treatments, but nothing had worked. The week they told me they were on some girls' trip they went to Texas to see a specialist. The cancer was to advance and there was nothing that could be done.

I broke all the way down. At first, I was angry because they kept it from me. Then I felt sad because I didn't want my grandma to die. Six months passed and on her 60th birthday she took her last breath. I don't think I ever felt so fucked up before and probably never would. Staci and Kaine gave my grandma a beautiful farewell and Staci cried her eyes out for my grandma. Tiff was right there for me every step of the way although I didn't make it easy. Once I snapped out of it I figured I would live life and try my best to make my old lady proud of me. I was so wrapped up in my thoughts I forgot I was still at her grave. Tiff was rubbing my back and shedding tears with me. This was why I loved her so much. We shared each other's pain. She was always so patient and let me be venerable with her without making me feel less of a man.

"Brandon, you know your grandma is very proud of you and always will be. I know you feel like you had all these plans with her. But God had better plans and she is at peace now. No more pain, no more hospitals and machines plugged up to her. I believe she is with you every step of the way in all you do. She's right here." Tiff pointed to my heart. She smiled at me, kissed my lips and then hugged me tight. We stood there just hugging and I felt a little better. Tiff wiped my tears and kissed me again. She turned and looked at my grandma's grave.

"Mrs. Will—I mean grandma. You did such a wonderful job with this man right here. I promise to take care of him." She smiled at my grandma's picture and I smiled at my wife. I grabbed her hand and we walked back to our truck. I helped Tiff in and I walked on the driver's side. Getting in I looked at Tiff's pretty ass face. She smiled at me and grabbed my hand.

"You ready for this brown sugar?" I asked her while squeezing her hand.

"Ready more then I'll ever be." I smiled at her response and leaned over to kiss her. I put the truck in drive and pulled off. We were headed to Tiff's parent's house to pick up Brandy. Once we got my squeak we were all on our way to our private plane and headed to Miami. It's been real Louisiana.

Two weeks later (Welcome to Miami!)

"Are you nervous about today?" Tiff asked me as I

got ready for tonight. That's right ya' boy had his own club in Miami. Karlos let me take two of our best dudes down here with me. They all were happy to get out of Louisiana and get promotions. I let them run the club with me and run a lot of our illegal shit also. The one thing me and my bros tried to always do was give our crew a chance to have a come up. some of them were born to be corner boys and some of them were more than that. It was our job to choose wisely. Tonight, wasn't my grand-opening, I was just going to see everything, meet the staff and make sure I'm satisfied.

"Naw I'm good. Travis and Cole have been down here two months before us. I trust they have done right with the details of the club. Will you and Brandy be good without me? I can stay home." I turned around and looked at Tiff. I was dead ass, fuck this club shit. If my wife needed me then I would stay here.

"Brandon, you have already put this off for two months. Me and Brandy will be fine bae. I promise." She fixed my chain and smiled at me. I looked at Brandy sleep in our bed and I looked back at my pretty wife.

"I love you brown sugar. You know that, right?" Tiff nodded, and I got mad.

"What the hell does the head nod mean Tiffany? Open that sexy ass mouth." I pulled the seam of her short ass pajama shorts and yanked her to me. I loved when Tiff wore her short pajama shorts because they hugged her round booty.

"You must be annoyed since you hit me with the whole government name. You know how I feel Bra----" I cut her ass off and lifted her up pressing her against the wall in our huge ass walk-in closet. Tiff liked that rough shit so she bit her lip and I bet if I put my hands in her shorts my hand would be soaked. But I couldn't do that because if I did I wasn't going anywhere tonight. Shit, I was already swelling up in my jeans.

"I don't know shit unless you tell me. You know I hate that head nodding shit. Now, open that sexy ass mouth and tell me how you feel." I had both my hands gripping her ass cheeks hard as fuck. Tiff loved that shit. She started grinding on my hard dick and I had to think of everything but her pussy.

"I love you Brandon, you my babe. Can I have a kiss?" See, Tiff liked fucking playing with me. She knew I had to go to work. She also knew her big ass lips were everything to me. Never being one to back down I kissed her. Them big ass lips of hers were juicy and wet. I still had her pinned against the wall with her legs in my arms. I pulled away and just looked at my sexy wife.

"Keep fucking with me Tiff and I swear I will fuck you silly when I get back. Put squeak in her bed and when I come home you better be naked." I kissed her on the lips and let her down. I walked away leaving her standing there horny. Tiff wasn't crazy, so she knew not to play with that pussy. Her ass better take a cold shower and wait for me. I went over to my squeak and kissed her on her chubby cheek. I grabbed my keys and left out our house.

**

I pulled up to my club looking like the boss I felt. We were not scheduled to open until Saturday but anything that was associated with my name had to be done right. This was not my first time seeing the inside of the club, so I was good on that. But I wanted to see all the dancers and make sure they were up to my standards. I wanted to have a variety of dancers for each itch a nigga had. I was in my black 2017 Ferrari F60 and parked it in the underground gated parking I had for employees. I wanted the dancers and bartenders to feel safe coming from work. You see my club was staffed with women only. Sex sells, and nothing was sexier than a club staffed with sexy ass women.

Tonight, I was here to meet the entire staff Travis and Cole picked out.

I was killin' the game with my all black Fendi short sleeve fitted t-shirt. My matching black faded Fendi jeans went well with my Dolce and Gabbana sneakers. I wanted to keep my jewelry simple, so my wrist froze with my custom Rolex and diamond studs. My waves in my head put the ocean to shame and my beard was trimmed. I looked at the name 'Legz written in big black and gold light up letters on the front of the club. I know that's a weird name but that's all you see when you step in my club. Sexy ass legs of all races and shapes and they all had sexy ass red bottoms to compliment them. Red bottoms which I provided and made them leave at work when they went home. Like I said, I wanted a different type of club.

I walked in the entrance and the seven big ass bouncers I had were all lined up by the door. They had there all black on with the Legz written in the front of their shirt and Security written on the back. I nodded my head at each of them and kept moving along. I looked at the empty club and smiled to myself. The shit was exactly how I imagined it to be! All black with glass walls, floors, ceiling and DJ booth. I had the long wrap around bar fully stocked with any liquor, wine and champagne you could think of. I want cheap and baller status drinks available. The black leather booths made the club look sexy and intimate. I didn't want a two and three-story club like Royalty. I wanted a one level club that was big as hell! Legz was a hundred and thirty-four thousand square feet. This was my new baby and I was proud of how she turned out.

"Boss man you finally here!" Travis came from the back with Cole behind him. We dapped each other up and chatted it up for a few minutes.

We talked to the security guards and told them their responsibilities any night we are open. Cole went to the intercom and called all the girls to the floor. They had already informed them that I would be here tonight so if you weren't present then you no longer worked at Legz. The girls came out and lined up. From what I could see the staff was all that and then some. But any bitch looked good under the right light. I stood up ready to look at each one from their legs to their teeth. I wasn't about to have a bitch working for me whose teeth looks like the signal bars on a damn phone.

After looking at all the girls I was pleased. I separated the dancers from the bartenders. If you weren't on stage or on the clock, then you were to be in heels. I can't front, Cole and Travis did good as fuck. They had two sexy ass plus size chocolate girls whose face was chiseled by God himself. I never discriminated! As long as their face was pretty as fuck, and they weren't sloppy with it, then I could get with it. Anyways, back to the bitches at hand. I looked at all the fat asses, nice size titties, flawless skin, nice teeth, good breath and even underarms smelled good. I looked at all the beautiful women and realized something was missing.

"Aye yo, why y'all ain't hire no snow bunnies? Y'all even got two blasian girls but no snow bunnies. This Miami, I know some bad ass white girls came in here." I looked at Cole and Travis and asked.

"I mean, they did come in, but my dick didn't get hard lookin' at them. They had chitterlings lookin' pussy." Travis said making all of us including the girls fall out laughing.

"Y'all niggas dumb! Come on man, hold another audition and get me at least three snow bunnies. No crystal meth lookin' white girls. I want Scarlett Johansson or Mila Kunis lookin' bitch with a black girl body." I told them taking my shot of henny.

"Nigga yo' ass wasn't here. When word got out you

owned a club and looking for female staff. The line was wrapped around the block. Every bitch that came in here asked about you and yo' brothers. Shit mad annoying nigga." Cole said. Me and Travis laughed, and Travis told me Cole wasn't lying.

"Ain't shit gone stop that nigga, my whole face smell like my wife's sweet ass crack and the bitches still flock. Just get my snow bunnies in this bitch." I took another shot and got to talking to the staff. I had to let the girls know the rules and what I expected out of them.

After talking to them I went to my office for a minute. I made sure everything was in order for Saturday. I sat at my desk and looked at my nice ass office. I had my shit all army green and black. I had a private full bathroom with a nice black wood desk, leather chair with a couch and love seat in front of a 60-inch TV. I couldn't wait to fuck Tiff in here just like I had her pop that pussy for me in my office at Royalty. After I made sure shit was good with everything I was ready to head out. It was going on midnight, so I knew my house was shut down, but Tiff was definitely about to wake her ass up though.

Tiff

I felt the covers slowly slide down my body. Turning my head, I saw Brandon standing over me naked with a hard dick. I smirked and looked from his dick to his sexy ass face. Brandon was 6'3 which towered over me. He was so chocolate with an athletic hard body that he kept toned as fuck. My name was big as hell written across his chest in big cursive letters. I looked at his right hand and saw he was holding a spreader bar. I licked my lips and my pussy got so wet. I knew I was getting dicked down, but I didn't think I was about to get all of this. I was happier than a kid in a toy store.

"Didn't I tell yo' ass to be naked?" He asked looking annoyed. I sat up on my knees.

"I am babe." I held both my arms out to show him my body. He still looked mad.

"Tiffany, what the fuck are those?" I looked down at my thin ass lace panties. They were tiny and barely noticeable. Brandon yanked me up with one arm and kissed me. I mean he kissed me deeper than a 10-inch pool. Still kissing me he let my arm go and with one hand he ripped my panties.

"You owe me a trip to Victoria Secret." He ignored me and pulled my ankles. I bit my lip when he strapped my ankles to the bar. Within seconds I was laying on my back flat on the bed with the bar between my legs. I was so damn horny and ready for all that Brandon had for me. His dick was so chocolate with a dark pink head. He had a little hair on his pelvis like I liked! I wish y'all could see how Brandon had my pussy contracting. She was calling out to him so loud that I felt wetness on my thighs.

"Look at na-na ready for me. I'm abusing her tonight

for you trying to tease me earlier. And for yo' ass not doing what I said about being naked." He yanked the bar between his legs dragging me down by the foot of the bed. I was breathing hard as hell because I loved how aggressive Brandon is. Every woman loved a nigga to have some aggression to him. Actually, the harder a bitch tries to act. The more she like to be man handled in a good way, not on no Ike and Tina shit.

Brandon leaned forward to my face, he sucked and licked on my neck. Then he kissed and sucked his way to my titties. I know no nigga walking this earth sucked titties better than Brandon. I had gone to get my nipples pierced on a dare with Kylee one day. I thought Brandon would be mad, but he loved it. Brandon started with my left titty and licked the entire thing. He bit and pulled on my nipples while having his hand flat on the bed. He had his other hand pinching and pulling on my other nipple. When he rolled my nipple between his teeth and tongue I came all over myself! Brandon looked down and looked back up at me with the sexiest look a nigga could give.

"Damn brown sugar, I love when I get you like that." He stood up and grabbed the bar. With one hand he flipped my entire ass over and made me get in doggy style. It was so smooth and took little effort. He hit both my ass cheeks as he dove in and ate my pussy from the back.

"Ugh shit babe! Eat this pussy Brandon! Make me cum!" Two hard slaps on the ass later and I was cumming like the rain on hurricane season. I felt sleep want to take over me after cummin' twice like I did. Only Brandon could make me cum without dick! And only Brandon could make me cum so hard that I felt drained.

"Hell naw, wake yo' ass up. I need that pussy Tiff." His sexy ass voice sat in my ear drums and my pussy woke me up. Brandon grabbed the bar and flipped me over like some flap jacks. He spread the bar as far as it could go. I was laying on my back with my legs spread so far apart my clit was on full display. I'm tellin' y'all, if you have never tried a spreader bar you need to get you one! The shit is fire!

Brandon's sexy ass body was on top of mines as he stuck his tongue in my mouth. I wanted so bad to wrap my legs around his waist, but I couldn't. The urge to touch him and not being able to made it more erotic. Brandon went back to sucking and licking on my titties only this time, he stopped before I was about to cum. When his big dick entered me I almost screamed for my mama. His dick felt so damn good and even though Brandy had stretched my pussy hole to the max. I still was not used to my husband's thick ass dick.

"Arghh fuck babe! Mmmmm!" I moaned as he grinded in me massaging my walls with his dick. My pussy gripped him like a nigga hanging from a cliff. I was in heaven!

"Damn yo' pussy is the best Tiff. This pussy gone always be mine, you hear me brown sugar. This belongs to me." Between his words and his dick, I came two times and Brandon ass still didn't cum. I could tell I was in for a long rest of the night and morning. I was up for the challenge though.

*

Two Days Later

"You ready to see pop-pop and grandma, huh baby girl?" I smiled and kissed Brandy's cheeks while putting her sandals on. She looked so cute in her jean shorts and spaghetti strap shirt. Brandon is going to be so annoyed. He hated her in fitted shirts, but I thought she looked so cute. Brandy has always been a chubby baby so everything she wore fit her. I never dressed my baby like a thot. We had enough of those in the world. I dressed her like the chubby, pretty baby girl that she was.

"Mommy bye-bye!" Brandy screamed and laughed. My heart warmed anytime she said mommy.

"We are about to leave as soon as your grandparents get here." I picked her up and we walked down stairs. I had on the same thing Brandy was wearing except my shorts were high rise and my shirt was a halter top. We both wore purple Jordan Retro 12's on our feet and our hair was in a high ponytail.

We walked down stairs in the kitchen. I could hear Brandon in his man cave playing his game. My parents' plane should have landed by now. I offered to pick them up from the airport, but they had rented a car. They were staying out here for four days. Those were going to be a long four days. It's all from love but they still can be a little much. You'll see when they get here. I placed Brandy in her chair and gave her some bananas and apple juice. We were going out to eat when my parents arrived. I went and grabbed me a snack too. I heard Brandon come from down the hall.

"Hey my squeak!" I turned around and watched Brandy's face light up when she looked at her daddy. The sight was so beautiful and sexy as far as Brandon goes. He was already so fine but when he was in daddy mode he was even more delicious.

"Tiffany why my baby got this tight shirt and shorts on. You want me to fuck you up." He walked towards me looking annoyed. I couldn't help but laugh at him.

"Brandon, she looks fine. She has meat on her she can't help that her clothes fit a little snug. As long as she doesn't look like she is squeezing in them then she's fine." I was about to walk around him, but he blocked me.

"Where you going without giving me my suga, huh brown sugar?" He bit his lips and gave me that sexy ass look. Brandy was busy eating her bananas. I looked at him and brought my lips to his. Brandon slipped his hand in the back of my pockets and pulled me closer. I melted in his chocolate arms. Our kiss was so deep we didn't break until someone cleared their throats. We both looked up and saw my parents standing there.

"Well I'm glad to see you leave your door open for anybody to come in and harm both my babies." My mama said smiling and walking towards us.

"Hi mommy! Hi daddy!" I smiled big and hugged her tight. She hugged me and hugged Brandon as well. My dad hugged us and hurried up to pick Brandy up. They adored her and adored Brandon. Aside from my mama's reservations towards because of his passed mistake. Hey, she was my mother first before she was his mother in-law.

"Hey my lady bug. Look at this gorgeous house!' My dad looked around with awe in his eyes. He turned to Brandon with his hand out.

"You did good son in-law, this home is beautiful." They shook hands and my dad patted Brandon on his shoulder a few times. Me and my mother smiled because they were bonding, and it was really good to see. Once upon a time my dad wanted to put Brandon in the ground for hurting me. But with time and my convincing, my dad came around.

"You don't have to thank me for doing my job. My brown sugar and baby girl will always be covered even if I'm dead." I looked at Brandon like he was crazy. My dad didn't know me by 'brown sugar. Brandon had no chill and said the shit like he was talking to me. My dad just chuckled. We talked for a few and showed them the rest of the house.

"Lady bug, why is Brandy eating and we are about to go out to eat?" My mom asked taking the bag of bananas from Brandy making her cry. I saw Brandon get an angry look on his face.

"Ma, she is just having a snack." I told her taking the bag out her hand and giving it back to Brandy.

"Snacks turns into fat and you have put a lot of that on my granddaughter already." She smiled at Brandy and squeezed her cheeks.

"Tilly shut the hell up!" My dad said with sternness in his voice. My mother acted like she was zipping her lips and held her hands up in surrender. Me and Brandon looked at each other and he mouthed the words 'One more time.' I shook my head because I knew he meant my mama had one more time to come for Brandy about her weight.

After we were done with the tour we went to go eat some food. We took my parents to Big Pink. Our second night here we had dinner here and it was so good. The weather was nice and hot, Miami was looking amazing. The sun bounced off the palm trees making the green sparkle. I loved seeing the people walk around and drive their sports cars. It wasn't home, but it was getting to be comfortable being here.

"No vegan meals for us! I think I want to get spaghetti and meatballs." My mama said, and Brandy laughed and tried to say spaghetti. They were sitting across from me and Brandon and Brandy was sitting on the end of the table next to me and my mom.

"Oh no baby girl. You weigh enough, salad for you." My mother said. Me and my dad looked at her like she was crazy.

"Fat or skinny my baby looks better than all these ugly ass kids in here." Brandon said to my mama looking annoyed. I closed my eyes and breathed in. I couldn't get mad at my husband because he was protecting our daughter. This is what I was talking about when I said my mama can be critical. I can take when she does it to me, but Brandy is a child.

"I'm not saying she is ugly I'm just sayin----"

"Some shit that don't need to be said. Look at your daughter and look at what we made. You couldn't see how perfect she is, but you damn will recognize how perfect Brandy is. That's my blood running through her as well. Both of them are as good as you get to being perfect." Brandon said pointing myself and Brandy. I smiled and so did my father. We loved my mama, but she had to be put in her place and Brandon was the person to do it. She always knew how to guilt me and my dad and make us feel bad.

"Well, I never felt so not wanted before. Maybe I should just leave early and you all can enjoy your father." She picked up her napkin like she was about to cry. My dad kept eating and playing with Brandy. I was about to give in, but Brandon rubbed on my thigh making me remember my mama's game. When none of us paid her any attention she gave up and started playing with Brandy. The rest of dinner was fun, we showed my parents Miami and then we drove them to Brandon's night club and my gym. My mama and dad were impressed and so happy for us.

"Lady bug, I am so proud of you and Brandon. You two have come together and built such an empire and I couldn't be happier for you. I apologize if I ever come off hard on you. I just want you guys to be around for a long time. I know eating right and staying fit will help with that." We were in the guest room in our house. Brandy was asleep, my dad and my sexy husband were in his man cave watching TV and smoking weed. Yea, my dad smoked weed!

"Mama, Brandy is one years old. I am not doing to her what you did to me. Now, I won't let her get unhealthy and I will monitor what I give her. But I will not make her feel uncomfortable or like she has to count carbs at the age of five. I love you and I know you mean well, but ease up off my baby. And off Brandon." I looked at her as I helped her put clothes in the drawer.

"I will lady bug, I promise. And I am not tough on Brandon. I just know what's walking up and down these Miami streets and in his dirty night club." My mama twisted her neck with an attitude.

"I know mama and I understand your skepticism. Believe me, I would be the same with Brandy. But ma, I love him, and he is my husband. I know my worth so trust me, the minute things would even try to go south me, and Brandy would go out the damn door. Trust me mama and know I got this." She walked up to me and hugged me. I loved my mama and I knew she meant well. I was just as nervous as she was. But my faith was with God and my husband. Until otherwise was shown then I had no choice but to trust.

Blair

"Bitch would you stop playing and tell me what you been holdin' out on?" I looked at Sarah while she clocked out after me. We both opened Wendy's together this morning, so we didn't have to close.

"Um I need y'all to open for the next two days. Joe and Cleo quit so until I get some more help it will be just the three of us." Melissa our fat ass manager told us. I couldn't stand her because she played favorites with us. Whoever kissed her ass for the week got the best schedule.

"Melissa, what's wrong with Ron and Tyrone closing?" I asked annoyed. Shit, they been here longer than us, so I knew they could open.

"You are worried about the wrong shit! Open or there is no place for you here anymore." She wobbled her short fat ass away.

"I hate her Danny Devito looking ass. Ron and Tyrone quit after she sucked both of their little ass dicks. I heard they were stealing too but she so fucking stupid she sucked them off anyways." I told Sarah as we walked outside. She started laughing as we both approached our cars. Sarah drove a 2017 Lexus from her nigga Smoke who was Raheem's best friend. Snake was nothing like Raheem. He was sexy like him, but he wasn't controlling at all nor did he cheat on her. In fact, he loved the ground Sarah walked on. I was happy for my girl, but I was jealous because I wanted what she had. Not with Smoke, I wanted Raheem to act like him. Even though Smoke took care of her, she still worked and went to school like I did. Raheem and Smoke had been best friends since they met in juvie. They were mad close and did everything together.

"Girl fuck her and this job. I'm ready to tell you the news I been saving." Sarah leaned against her door. I put my hands on my hips waiting for her to talk.

"I found out a new hot club is opening up here and they are looking for some dancers. Now, here me out before you shut me down." Sarah smiled big as hell.

"Bitch spill it, it's too hot to be standing out here with you playin'." I was getting annoyed by her dragging the news. She was right about me shutting her down though. Hell, neither one of us were dancers. Sarah started laughing at me.

"Impatient hoe! Anyways, Brandon Royal owns the club bitch. My girl from my wine and paint class told me he moved here. You remember Brandon right, you fell for his ass after sucking his dick." Sarah teased me and started laughing.

I was standing there stuck on stupid. I had put that name and face far behind me. He was the first nigga I ever gave head to just off conversation. I don't know what made me do it I just wanted some of his chocolate ass any way that I could. He told me off rip he had a woman but what nigga would turn down head from a bad bitch. Besides the bomb head I laid on him, our conversation was dope as fuck. We vibed so good and I know he felt something too. Because even after he nutted all down my throat, we chilled together the rest of the night and the next day he hit me up. We went to lunch and had more good convo and we ended up in a hotel room. Where I gave him some more head and we fucked. I wanted to kiss his juicy lips and feel his tongue on my pussy. But he shut all that shit down and told me only his woman gets that privilege.

I felt some type of way, but I let it go because I didn't want to fuck up what we had. Brandon's dick was so good! I know for a fact no nigga would ever, ever, ever fuck me like he did. When he went back to Louisiana he acted like I didn't exist. He ignored my texts, calls and DMs. But he posted a million pics of him and his bitch trying to act like he was just so happy and faithful. So, me being the typical bitter bitch at that time. I told his woman about us. I didn't spill all the beans and tell her I rode his dick for about an hour. I told her I gave him some head at their kick back in Miami. I also showed her the texts he sent me about keeping what we did on the DL.

The next thing I knew, he was calling me going off and threating me. I felt bad because he cut me off from all communications. He blocked me from everything and really treated me like I didn't exist. I could have made fake pages and called him from other numbers. But a few weeks later I met Raheem and he took all my attention from Brandon. Raheem was just as fine and dick was almost just as good, so I put Brandon out my head. Now, he lives here, and my best friend wanted to work at his club.

"Blair, Blair! Damn bitch, you don't hear me talking to you?" Sarah yelled at me. I turned my nose up at her loud mouth ass. Sarah was white but she had an inner black girl inside of her. Not only was her body built like ours, she talked like us too and only dated black guys. He parents are the typical suburban married couple. But Sarah's mama's father was black and Sarah inherited all the good ass benefits of being black. She was thick with wide hips, a flat stomach, a round big booty and breast that she bought when she turned nineteen.

"You got such a loud mouth bitch. I heard yo' annoying ass I was in deep thought." I smirked at her. She laughed and flipped her long black hair.

"I bet you were in deep thought. You want some more of that Royal dick don't you? That's why we should audition to work there. We both are bad as fuck and can twerk good as fuck. We might as well get paid for it. Auditions are at eight o' clock tonight and we are going." Sarah told me. I was all for it until someone popped in my head.

"Bitch, I gotta do some serious dick sucking if I am going to get Raheem to agree with this." I told Sarah. She rolled her eyes and laughed.

"So, you mean to tell me you're not even a little anxious to see Brandon?" Sarah asked me as I took out my phone to text Raheem. I looked up at her and smacked my lips.

"Girl no, I mean it's going to be nice to see his black skinny ass but I want the job more than I want to see him. We could make in one night what we make at this piece of shit." I pointed to Wendy's. Sarah twisted her lips up and laughed.

"Yea whatever bitch! You can front all you want but I know you wanna see him. Give me a hug bitch I gotta go. Be ready at seven o'clock I'm coming to get you. Tell Raheem don't make me beat his ass." I hugged my best friend and we both got in our cars. I looked at my phone and saw Raheem sent a picture of his hard dick again. I smiled and pulled out the Wendy's parking lot headed home to sit on that big dick.

*

"Raheem, I need to ask you something boo." I was drawing circles with my nail on my index finger on his chest. We had just had a good ass fuck session and I knew this was the best time for me to bring up this dancing thing. I had no idea how this was going to turn out but I had a plan with how I wanted to sell this.

"Ask me whatever you want angel face." He had his legs in tangled with mines and his hands were in my hair. When he was like this, you forgot how controlling and scary he could be.

"So, Melissa is firing me and Sarah. She wants to bring in two of her sisters and her payroll only is for two of us out the four. Of course, she is giving us the boot. You know that fat bitch has always hated me and Sarah.

Anyways, Sarah found out that this new club is looking for dancers and bartenders." I laid there on his chest. I was still and held my breath waiting for him to respond. All of a sudden Raheem grabbed my neck and flipped me over with him on top. He had that familiar crazy look in his eyes. He wasn't gripping my neck as hard as he was when we fell out a few weeks ago. But it still was a tight grip.

"So, let me get this bullshit straight. You tryna show off my fucking goods to niggas so they can put money in yo' fuckin' G-string. Niggas greasy, slimy ass hands will be all over what fucking belongs to me! Are you fucking stupid Blair! You belong to me, you my fuckin' property! No nigga will be looking at you or fantasizing about you." He bit his lip and tried to squeeze harder, but I remained calm and rubbed his face. His grip loosened, and he just looked at me.

"Raheem, look what you just said. I belong to you, therefore I don't give a fuck about who looks at me or wants me. I only want you. I only care about you looking at me. Plus, didn't you tell me about the police being hot on you and your crew? If I worked at the club that's a guaranteed profit and a way to secure that we will always have money. I'm doing this for us boo." I looked in his eyes with the sincerest I have ever looked. Raheem smiled and kissed me deep. I was happy as fuck that he bought what I was selling. I knew if I mentioned the police and money he would see things my way.

"I swear I am going to marry you one-day angel face. You're always looking out for me and putting us first. I apologize for acting crazy on you I just don't want you to slip through my fingers. I wanna give you the world angel face and as long as you keep following my rules, then we are always going to be good. If this club shit is a way for you to change up on a nigga. I swear I will kill yo' ass." He looked at me with menace in his eyes as he stroked my face. His eyes went to my nose, mouth and entire face as if he was examining me.

"I would hate to kill a face this angelic, but I will if you ever thought about doing life without me." He kissed me again and for the first time since being with him. I was fearful for my life. I had to figure out how to take control of this situation. I know Raheem could be the perfect nigga if he just understands the control shit is not ok. My mind went to tonight and the fact that I was going to see Brandon. I swear I hope he doesn't let our past determine if he would hire me or not. His boney ass better let that shit go like I did and put me on the payroll.

     **

"Bitch why is this line filled with white bitches?" I whispered to Sarah as we stood in line inside of the club. I was the only "sista" in the damn room and that seemed pretty odd to me.

"I don't know, maybe it's a coincidence." Sarah shrugged her shoulders. I smacked my lips and looked around.

"Bitch, coincidence my ass. I think it's only white girl's they are looking for. I'm out of here." I was about to leave but Sarah grabbed my arm and told me to stay. I blew out my mouth and rolled my eyes. Clearly Brandon's ass wanted a club filled with white bitches. Fucking sell out!

"Ok ladies. We need dancers who can work the stage, work the floor and who can work the pole. If you need lessons on the pole, then I can work with you. If you are rhythm-less and stiff, get the fuck out." Some sexy ass black girl spoke to us. She had two other fine ass black guys standing next to her.

"These are the owners Cole and Travis. They are here to look at you with their dick. If you don't wake their dick up, then you're not for Legz. Let's get to it." The sexy chick, Cole and Travis went to sit down in front of the stage. The girls started going up on the stage with their choice of music. Some went up there solo, others went up there as a pair. The guys were ruthless to the girls who couldn't dance or looked like shit. The nigga named Cole told one girl she had a wrinkled pussy. I tried not to laugh because I didn't know how good me and Sarah were going to be. Speaking of our name, that's what we forgot. Stage names.

"Bitch what are we going to call ourselves. We can't get up there and say our government name." I whispered to Sarah as some white girl was killing it on the pole. I never took white strippers serious, but this bitch was killing it. She was dancing to Chris Brown Privacy song and she was killin' it.

"Don't worry about that bestie, I got you. Remember that threesome we did for my ex Quay? Remember the Shakira and Beyoncé thing we did?" She asked me and I smiled big as fuck. That's why she had me wear this long, skin tight black halter dress. She matched me and we both had on a black G-string and black red bottom pumps that strapped around the ankle. We gave her ex-boyfriend a threesome for his birthday. The shit was all the way live and we had so much fun when we made his Shakira and Beyoncé fantasy come true. It was our turn and Sarah gave the DJ the cd she picked.

"Um this audition called for snow bunnies only." The bad chick said to us. I held my breath hoping Sarah could get her to change her mind.

"I know but I never do anything without my Peppa. We are the shit together and if you just see our routine you can decide for yourself." Sarah grabbed my hand and squeezed it. I looked at them and the nigga Cole was eye fucking me so hard I felt pregnant. They talked, and the bad chick nodded her head. Soon enough Shakira and Beyoncé's song Beautiful Liar played through the speakers.

He said I'm worth it, his one desire
I know things about 'em that you wouldn't wanna read
about
He kissed me, his one and only, (yes) beautiful Liar
Tell me how you tolerate the things that you just found out
about
You never know
Why are we the ones who suffer
I have to let go
He won't be the one to cry

I lay down on my back with the pole between my legs. Sarah climbed up the pole and slid down sexy as fuck. She landed in the split form on top of me. Moving her body like a snake on top of mine I grabbed the bottom of her dress. Sarah did a tumble very slow from on top of me coming out of her dress the same time she did the tumble. It was so sexy and smooth I could see the guys looking at her sexy ass body like she was gold. Now Sarah was laying on her back. I crawled seductively to her and climbed on top of her body. I started hip rolling on top of her. Our skin mixed together looked like a smooth melted marshmallow on top of a melted Hershey's bar. Sarah pulled my dress over my head and like a nigga, she flipped me over on my back and started grinding on top of me.

Let's not kill the karma
(Ay) Let's not start a fight
(Ay) It's not worth the drama
For a beautiful liar
Can't we laugh about it (Ha Ha Ha)
(Oh) It's not worth our time
(Oh) We can live without 'em
Just a beautiful liar

We both were doing the splits and hip rolling at the same time. I kept eye contact on the nigga that was eye fucking me. I swear I saw his dick print from the stage. Even the bad chick was turned on watching us. I put my face by Sarah's ass while she slowly twerked each ass cheek to the beat. I was doing the same thing as I slicked the top of her left ass cheek. She looked back at me and smiled. When we were done the three of them were fucking speechless.

"Well got damn y'all! That shit was live just like you said. So, since she's Peppa you must be Salt?" The bad chick asked Sarah. We both were standing up in just a G-string and pumps. Our perky titties on full display.

"That's right! We could work together and make y'all hella fucking money!" Sarah was really selling us. The three of them talked for a second and smiled at us.

"A few pole dancing lessons and we have a deal. I want more routines together like that, all slow songs. That will be y'all thing." Me and Sarah smiled and picked up our dresses. They discussed some more details with us and told us we needed to work on grand-opening night. I was so geeked up.

"I thought you said Brandon Royal owned this club. The chick said those two guys owned it." I told Sarah as we walked to her car. I was on a high after we killed the audition and got the job.

"I guess it was just a rumor. Anyways, fuck him girl we got the job! We can tell Melissa to kiss out perfectly shaped asses!" Sarah screamed and started twerking. I laughed as I texted Raheem that we got the job and I was on my way home.

"Hell yea! I'm wiping my ass with a Wendy's napkin and throwing it at her." I laughed and high fived Sarah. We got in the car and headed towards my place. I was so happy I didn't have to see Brandon after all. I guess life worked out in my favor because I doubt he would have hired me. Now to stack this money and get my nigga to act right. Life was going to be sweet as fuck!

Brandon

(The grand Opening)

If your dude come close to me
He gon' want to ride off in a Ghost with me
(I'll make him do it!)
I might let your boy chauffeur me
But he gotta eat the booty like groceries
But he gotta get rid of these hoes from me
I might have that nigga selling his soul for me
Ooh, that's how it post to be
If he wants me to expose the freak
Ooh, that's how it post to be
Everything good like it post to be

Jhene Aiko had all the ladies singing her part on Omarion hit Post to Be. Tonight, was the grand opening of Legz and as I looked around my live ass club, I felt satisfied as fuck. Earlier today my bros and their wives surprised me and Tiff. They showed up early this morning at the house. They were here for the rest of the week and I couldn't be happier. I thought they asses was all busy, so I didn't think they were coming. I was like a bitch in my feelings which I would never tell they asses. Tiff was happy as fuck that her crew was here. The way they had my house turned upside down felt just like old times. We were in VIP partying shit up and enjoying life.

"Bro this shit is fuckin' poppin my nigga! I'm proud of yo' ass." Karlos dapped me up and gave me a brotherly hug. He always pulled out the 'pops' hat whenever we accomplished some shit. We lowkey ate that shit up though.

"Thanks bro! I'm glad y'all were able to come out and celebrate with us." I told him while he took his Henny shot.

We were all getting wasted and some of us were smoking. Kim was the only one not drinking. She was pregnant as hell with her and Kevin's son. He didn't want her to come but he didn't want to leave her alone. His ass was watching her like a hawk. Me and my bros had the baddest women on our arms and like always they were looking good as fuck. Tiff wore this black fitted dress. It was long and had her whole back out to the top of her ass. I wanted to bend her over in my office. She had her black hair in that blunt cut I love that stopped at her shoulders. Something about her big lips in that red lipstick was making me want to shove my dick down her throat. Brandy was staying at the house with my in-laws and me and Tiff got a suite. I was definitely breaking her off when we got up out of here. If she keeps dancing on me like she is doing then it might be sooner. My three-piece Armani suit was matching Tiff's black dress. We both were dripped in diamonds.

Looking at my club filled with people was making me feel like the boss I already was. The staff looked good as fuck and even the snow bunnies that were hired looked good as fuck too. Cole told me they hired more than I said because they wanted to make some of them servers. I was cool with it and from the looks of shit they chose wisely. The stage was filled with bad bitches shaking what they mamas gave them. We had trash bags filled with money and we let our wives throw it at the strippers. The shit was sexy as fuck watching Tiff get a lap dance by this thick ass Spanish bitch. Tiff made it rain on her and my dick almost broke off of me and jumped in Tiff's pussy. The girls walked back over to us and we continued to party.

The lights dimmed, and the DJ announced a special

performance. Travis told me they found a for sure money maker the day they held auditions. I was eager to see what the show was going to be like. The red light on the stage looked sexy as fuck with the mirrors and mirrored floors. 6LACK PRBLMS came on and a sexy ass thick snow bunny came sliding down the pole. She was bad as fuck. Her body looked like a black girl body and the way her ass shook I could tell it was real. He had on some clear stripper heels and a red thong bikini.

And she said
You a God damn lie
I ain't mean to say that shit girl I was God damn high
So we left the crib now we in the God damn ride
She lookin' God damn fine
I wanted a bitch who was down to Earth
But she want the God damn skies
List of my problems
Got this one on my line that won't stop fucking callin'
It's crazy I made her that way

The way she worked the pole and moved had every nigga in here mesmerized. Then on the second part of the song she laid down flat and another bad, thick brown-skin girl came twirling down the pole. She landed in split position on top of the snow bunny. She had the same color bikini on as the white girl. They danced seductively all over each other. When the took their biking tops off four of the bounciest titties I have ever seen were shown.

This shit made you believe all the equality shit Martin Luther King Jr preached about. No disrespect at all but oh my fucking goodness that vanilla and chocolate swirled together looked so damn good. The brown skin baddie crawled towards the end of the stage. When I tell y'all a nigga almost shot fire out of my fucking head. I couldn't believe who the fuck I was looking at. The bitch Blair who I cheated on Tiff with was in my fucking club. Dancing on my stage and on my fucking payroll. Who the fuck in the heavens did I piss off. I felt my whole demeanor change and of course Tiff noticed.

"You ok babe, they got you that hot and bothered?" She smiled and kissed my lips. I had to play the shit off. The only thing that was saving me was the fact that Tiff never knew what Blair looked like. She never even knew her real name. Blair made a fake account named Michelle when she contacted Tiff. I knew Tiff had no clue because my wife and her crew would have dragged Blair off the stage.

"I'm good brown sugar I'm just hot and fuck in this suite and vest. Let me go holla at Cole for a minute I'll be right back." I kissed my brown sugar on the lips and walked towards my office.

I told Cole to send the Peppa bitch they named who danced with the white girl to my office. I made sure to tell him not to let her know it was me who wanted to see her. I walked in my office and waited for her to come in. I was so fucking heated because I don't know what she was up to. I swear if she was here to do more damage I sure enough was going to kill her tonight. I never told Tiff about what all went down with me and Blair. I know y'all cussin' a nigga out but I just couldn't tell her. Tiff would have left me for good if she knew I saw Blair after she sucked me off. I fed the hoe and fucked her after the party.

I don't know why I did it to tell you the truth. It was something about the way we vibed and let's not forget she is drop dead sexy. I wasn't about to leave my girl for nobody and I made that shit clear. That's why I was shocked how Blair switched up on me and got clingy. Any other time I would have gotten to know her better, but I was already taken. As I waited for her to come to my office I just hope she didn't say shit that would make me show my ass. A light tap came to my door and I told them to come in. I was in front of my desk leaning on it with my arms folded. When Blair stepped in and closed the door she looked at me like I was the grim reaper. I stared back at her and there was no denying her fucking beauty. She had a white tube dress and red bottoms that I provided on. Her hair was in a high ponytail.

"What the fuck are you doing here?" I asked her calmly still standing in the same position and looking at her. I could tell her breathing had changed. She had no fucking clue I was even here. She still looked at me with her mouth agape and her eyes bucked.

"Open yo' fuckin' mouth or I swear you are not walking up out of here." I said that shit with gritted teeth. She was fine and all but if she was coming to get between me and mine I had no problem with killing her ass.

"B-B-Brandon I didn't know-----"

"BULLSHIT! Don't fucking play with me Blair I swear this ain't what'chu want!" I looked at her fidget with her fingers. I swear I heard her heart beat fast over the loud music.

"Brandon, I swear I'm not lying. My best friend is the one I was dancing with. She told me you opened a club here and was looking for dancers. I wasn't going to even audition but she begged me, so I did. When we came and danced these two guys named Cole and Travis said they were the owners. I figured it was just a rumor about you owning this club, so I accepted the job." I looked at her as she talked, and I could tell she wasn't lying. I still didn't want to fuck around with it.

"Well now you are about to quit this muthafucka. I can't have you working here Blair. You too fuckin' messy. I brought my family here to start a new beginning. Not get wrapped up in some old ass drama. Sorry baby girl but you gotta get the fuck on. And if you think about causing a scene I will personally end yo' ass." I walked in front of her. I wasn't in her face, but I was close enough that she knew not to fuck with me.

"Brandon, I understand where you're coming from. I did some foul shit when we last saw each other. But I was young minded and lonely as fuck when I first got to Miami. I made us to be something more than what it was. I'm not with all that extra drama shit no more. I really need this job. I'm in school, have bills and boy—I mean my home life requires I have a job." Blair pleaded with me. I noticed she was about to say something else, but she caught herself. I stood there just looking at her in deep thought. Her face had a pleading look and her eyes were watering. I felt bad and against my better judgement I gave in.

"Blair, I swear I will bury you. Just come here, do you job and go the fuck home. One sneaky thing you try to do it's lights out baby girl." She wiped her eyes and nodded her head. Slowly she smiled and said.

"I swear to God Brandon, you get no drama from me." Blair held her hand up and crossed her heart. I laughed and rubbed my beard.

"Man, you should have saw my face when I recognized who the fuck you were. I didn't know yo' ass danced." She smiled big and because my tension eased away so did hers.

"I didn't even see you from the stage. I probably would have ran out the club like Diamond did when she saw her teacher in The Players Club movie." We both laughed when she said that reference.

"But for real Brandon, I work here and nothing else. I swear you won't regret this." She smiled big and turned to leave out my office. I breathed a small sigh of relief. I swear I didn't come to Miami to get a body under my belt. Hell, I had plenty of them but never for this reason. But then again, what good enough reason to kill somebody that tried to come between me and my brown sugar.

Tiff

"I don't know why you didn't want a grand opening Tiff. You know that shit would have been live as fuck." Brandon told me while I put my running shoes on. I was getting dressed for my first day at the gym I co-owned with Karlos.

"I told you I didn't want one and I didn't need one. It's already out there and were booked through the summer." I said it with confidence.

All I had to do was promote my gym along with the address. I did some YouTube videos from inside there a few months back. YouTube was big now and what better way to promote then that. I also did some Live videos with some of the instructors and a tour of what we had to offer. I told Karlos to do a gym with yoga, pilates, pole dancing classes and dance classes. Everybody was into all that shit especially the pole dancing classes. We had three famous chorographers who booked us all summer. Cash would stay flowing through this gym. The classes were first sign up first serve. Today was the first day and all the classes were filled including my yoga class. What made today even more special was my sisters were here to be with me on my first day. Kaylin and Kelly left two days ago to attend to the newborns. The rest of them were here for two more days. My parents left this morning, so Brandon had Brandy.

"I love yo' cocky ass attitude. Own that shit brown sugar." Brandon kissed me on the neck and squeezed my thighs. I had on some PINK yoga pants and my PINK muscle tank top.

"Stop kissing on my neck babe, you know I gotta leave." He started biting and sucking on it harder. If I closed my eyes, then it was a wrap.

"Oh, my goodness, get a fucking room." Kimmora yelled from the kitchen hallway. Me and Brandon laughed and went in the kitchen to join them. Kim was annoyed because Kevin wasn't letting her go to my gym with us. Her belly was huge so I couldn't blame him.

"Baby sis let me find out you hatin' when you and Kevin fucked in my damn office." Kimmora's whole face looked flushed. We fell out laughing and Kevin put his arms around her waist and laughed as well.

"Yea, yo' little ass thought y'all was being discreet. I didn't even break Tiff off in there yet! Fuckin' nasty asses." Brandon fell out laughing. Kimmora covered her face in shame laughing.

"I'm sorry Bran-Bran, he made me do it." She pointed to Kevin and threw his ass under the bus.

"That pregnant pussy be pullin' at me. Aye, we didn't touch shit though. I fucked her standing up against the door." Kevin's nasty ass said.

"Ayeeee shut up!" We all laughed and yelled at him.

"We don't need no details nigga!" Karlos' deep ass voice roared from behind Kylee. They were standing up eating off each other's plate. When I tell y'all they were glued together I mean that shit. But it was cute as hell though. Who would have thought, if y'all knew the old Karlos--- You know what, let me hush. That's another story for another book.

"Nigga shut yo' ass up! You and Kylee fuck in every vehicle y'all get in. Including when we rent party busses and limos." Kevin said. I laughed hard because it was the funniest thing hearing them go back and forth. Karlos and Kylee gave Kevin the middle finger.

"Ok babe we gotta get out of here. Let me kiss my baby girl good bye." I went and kissed Brandy in her high chair. She started looking sad but I had to ignore her because mama had to work. Kylee and Karlos kissed like they were never going to see each other again. Keira had to pull her ass from him.

"You nervous sis?" Keira asked me from the back seat. I decided to keep it simple and drive my Cadillac CTS. It was already hot out, so I had the A.C. on full blast.

"I am a little but I more excited to manage more than my class." I smiled hard as we drove laughing and talking like always.

We got to the gym and I almost jumped out the car before putting the gear in park. I was that damn excited. When I came in I saw the choregraph classes already in session. The dancers were going on tour with a few musicians. The pilates class for the mommy's expecting started already. I peeked in on each room and smiled big. My room was set up for me, but I was a half an hour early. I know, I was that excited!

"Hey Tiff!" Laura came from the back and hugged me. I met her a few months before we got out here. She was the designer to Karlos' first gym. She lived out here in Miami so I thought it was cool to see if she wanted to be an assistant manager. I couldn't be here every day and her schedule was open. I was excited when she agreed. She was a workout guru just like myself and she was gorgeous. Males would flock in here and pay for boxing lessons we had in the basement just for the fuck of it.

"Hey girl! I see everything is looking good and the classes are filled up. You did an amazing job opening up and setting up.

The bulletin was up and had all the classes we offered. The instructor's name and picture was up as well as their contact information. The vending machines and smoothie bar was stocked and ready. The whole gym colors were yellow and hot pink accept the basement. I had those colors black and red. You know guys do not want to be in a pink and yellow room. I had energy drinks and vending machines in the basement. Me, Kylee and Keira walked around seeing everything all set up. We walked in the female locker room and of course they were empty. Assuming the men's locker room would be empty we walked in there. I loved how I had both of the locker rooms designed. When we turned the corner to enter we saw a fucking God standing ass naked and soaking wet. I know we should have turned around and left. But the three of us were frozen. He was so damn fine with chocolate skin, long braids and a dick that made my knees buckle. He had on three dog tags around his neck and his body was on some other shit. I wanted to put his ass out for being so fine!

"We shouldn't be watching him. We're married to the craziest niggas in the fuckin' world." Kylee said but still kept her eyes on the chocolate God.

"Bitch you the one with the crazy husband. You need to leave before his Kylee's radar turns on and he kills us all." Keira whispered back to Kylee. We all still stood there watching him.

"You're right, I should go." Kylee said but still not moving.

"Just a few more seconds." She said while biting her lip. We stood there still watching him like the pervs we were

Kylee's loud ass phone rung Ashanti's Baby song. She tried to shut it off and we all tried to leave but bumped into each other. Kylee's phone dropped and I fell on my ass running into Keira. I crawled out with the quickness with Keira crawling behind me. Kylee's big booty ass ran and left us. I pray to God that man did not catch our creep asses staring at him. When we got far from the locker room Kylee was cracking up at us while putting her battery back in her phone.

"You ain't shit Kylee, how you gone leave us?" I was now cracking up breathing hard as fuck. Keira was still on the floor laughing. Kylee was laughing so hard she couldn't even put her phone together.

"Shit I panicked when I heard Karlos' ringtone go off. I think his ass does have Kylee radar. Y'all jinxed me." Pointing her finger at us and laughing she paused.

"Oh my God." She started whispering. Keira stood up to see what me and Kylee was looking at. The fine mystery guy walked out the locker room. I looked at his picture and realized he was the boxing instructor. He looked our way and winked before making his way downstairs.

"Got damn he fine as fuck." Kylee said as the three of us watched him go to the basement. Ashanti's voice snapped us out of thought. Swear Karlos had a chip planted on Kylee that told him when a nigga was in a mile radius of her.

"Girl, answer before his ass pops up with guns blazing." Keira said, and we started laughing. Kylee put the middle finger up to us.

"Hey my Los." She answered and began talking to him. I realized I needed to get ready for my yoga class.
*

My first class went very well, it was a breeze to teach because yoga was something I did as a morning ritual. The only thing that had me nervous was the sixteen people in class waiting for me to take lead. Oh, did I mention fine naked guy joined my class? Kylee and Keira looked just as shocked as I was. He put his mat next to Kylee and Keira who was directly in front of me. Keira's red ass turned red and Kylee kept giggling. I was ready to slap both of my sisters. When the class was over he rolled up his mat and left with the rest of the class. Before he winked at me! I read his contact information and learned his name was Quan. He's an army vet and a light weight boxing expert. He had pictures with Floyd Mayweather, Mike Tyson and the famous Muhammad Ali in 2014 before he passed away. Even then Mr. Quan was still fine and built nice.

"Are you learning about your new admirer?" Laura stood next to me and said. I was standing in front of the bulletin.

"Um no and what do you mean admirer? I don't even know him." I said nervously as I fixed my bag on my shoulder. I was waiting for Kylee and Keira to come out the locker room.

"Mmmhmm he was in here reading fun facts about you to before he left." She smirked and used air quotes when she said that. I laughed and thank God I was brown skin because I know I was blushing.

"Look, I know your married but it's nothing wrong if you have an admirer or if you think he is hot. Shit your married, not dead." Laura said and we both shared a laugh.

Kylee and Keira came out with their change of clothes. I they were staying in with me all day and we wanted to check out the pole dancing class. Laura worked the front desk and then she was going home to leave me to lock up. The three of us walked in the pole dancing class. It was the only class that had blackout windows. I didn't want niggas looking in getting a free show. I let the head dancer at Brandon's club Solo rent out this room every other day. I watched her in action and to me she needed to be on tour with Janet or Beyoncé. Not at a damn strip club but to each its own. I don't mind her making me and Brandon's pockets fat. Solo loved pussy so I didn't have to warn her about Brandon. Let me stop lying, I still warned her ass! Ha!

"We have a special, guest. The owner of this gym has decided to join us!" Solo announced me as me Kylee and Kiera entered the room.

Her eyes lit up when she looked at Kylee. Her slow ass didn't notice it but me and Keira caught on. I smiled and waved at the pretty ass girls who were in the room. There were some pretty BBW's in here too and I was proud as fuck. In my eyes BBW's were killin' the game and just as sexy as a slim bitch. Me, Kylee and Keira were putting our heels on when two girls walked in and immediately I recognized them as the dancers Salt and Peppa that danced at the grand-opening the other night. The three of us stood up ready to get started. When I tell y'all I thought this shit would be a breeze. I couldn't have been more wrong the shit was a real work out and you actually sweated. Keira mastered the shit like a damn pro and it had me and Kylee side eyeing her ass.

Rihanna Sex With Me song played as we did the routine Solo showed us. When I climbed up all the way on the pole my scary ass thought I was going to fall. But I did what Solo said and managed my weight and slid down with my legs around it. I felt sexy as hell after doing this class and I for sure would be back. Class was over and I was wiping my face and neck with my towel. Kylee was doing the same and Keira was taking her heels off. I saw the white and black girls who danced come our way.

"Hi, Solo told us you're the owner of this gym." The white girl said. The black girl kept looking at me and every time I looked back at her she would hurry and look away. I don't know why she would be nervous or scared to look at me. I ain't no damn body famous or nothing so who knew why she was acting all nervous.

"Yea that's me. I'm Tiff, these are my sisters Kylee and Keira." They spoke to each other.

"I'm Sarah and this is my best friend Blair. We both just wanted to come over and speak and tell you this gym is all the way live. How can I sign up for the choregraph class? I didn't see anything on the bulletin on how to." She asked me.

"Oh, that is a space rented out by some choreographers who just need the space. There not open for enrollment." I responded and nodded my head.

"Y'all two did a hell of a show the other night." Kylee said to them. The both of them smiled and thanked her. We talked for a few even though Blair barely spoke they still seemed like ok girls. They left out and I we stayed behind to help Solo clean up.

"So, Kylee do you live here to or just visiting?" Solo asked her. Me and Keira smirked because she was really hitting on Kylee and our poor sister had no clue.

"Naw, I'm just visiting sis for a few days. Tomorrow is my last, I'm from Louisiana." Kylee sweetly answered. Solo bit her lip and said.

"Too bad, when you come back to Miami you should chill with me." She grabbed Kylee's hand and winked at her while walking out. Kylee stood there looking stunned while me and Keira cracked up.

"Did she just?" Kylee still looked shocked as she turned and looked at me and Keira laughing.

"Hell yea she did sis! She wants the pussy!" Keira said cracking up. Kylee wrapped her towel around her body and turned her nose up.

"Bitch I'm not coming back to your gym. You got dykes hittin' on me, niggas naked slangin' dicks." She said shaking her head and walking out the room. Me and Keira was laughing so hard we were leaning up against each other to make sure we didn't fall over. Today was definitely a good day!

<u>Blair</u>

UGHH! This was ridiculous! I could not get comfortable for the life of me. It was midnight and I was trying to go to sleep. Every time I closed my eyes I saw Brandon's sexy ass face. The shit got so bad that I began getting scared to close my eyes. His sexy ass chocolate face was like a damn dream and I never wanted to wake up. The thing that really tripped me out was how big he has gotten. He never was small, but he wasn't that chiseled and muscular. That three-piece suit he had on made me want to peel it off of him. Even though he was threating my life I still couldn't look past how fucking gorgeous he was. Thoughts back to our sex came to my mind. I bet the sex was even better if we were to fuck now.

I swear when I walked in that office I thought I was going to meet Travis. I thought he either was going to hit on me, or I had did something wrong on stage and he was about to check my ass. When I opened that door, and ssw Brandon standing there staring back at me I almost died. I had put him back completely out my mind especially when he wasn't at the audition. And to top it all off, he watched me dance! He saw my body and saw me putting on a show for all of Miami. And as if God wasn't fucking with me already. His wife owns the gym me and Sarah take our pole dancing lessons at. Solo said we were really good on stage, but we need more practice on the pole.

Sarah is so fucking messy, when I told her I saw Brandon that night we snuck over on the low and saw him in VIP. The rest of the Royal brothers were there as well looking so damn sexy. Sarah lusted over Karlos the rest of the night. Even though he was all over his bitch. One of the dancers told us that they all were married now and with kids including Brandon. When I saw him with his wife I would be lying if I said they didn't look good together. The two of them needed to be in GQ magazine or on a damn runway together. The diamonds he had her and himself dripped in was my college tuition times three.

When we saw them at the pole dancing class I almost shitted myself. I didn't need Brandon thinking I was trying anything funny. As fine as he was, I believed all the threats he had given me that night at the grand-opening. Sarah thought it would be a good idea to make nice with Tiff to see what she was all about. I didn't want to go over there but there was no stopping Sarah once she was on a mission. I hated that Tiff was so cool and nice. Part of me wanted her to be a bitch or stuck up. That way I wouldn't feel bad about what I was feeling for her husband.

Tomorrow night I have to work, and I just hope Brandon won't be there. Bitch bye, we need to see him! That wetness and sensation we felt when we laid eyes on him was something else. That shit needs to happen again. My pussy had a mind of her own and she wanted to see Brandon. Hell, if it was up to her she'd do more than see him. Laying there looking at the ceiling, I heard the front door open downstairs. I knew it was Raheem, he had some business to handle tonight. I didn't even realize I'd been laying here for three straight hours.

"Hey angel face, why are you laying in the dark?" Raheem asked when he turned the light on and saw me laying here.

"I couldn't sleep." I rolled over on my side to look at him. Raheem was so fine there was no denying that. But he was so fucked up.

"You needed yo' daddy next to you. I missed yo' ass just as much." He said as he took off his shirt. His chocolate body was staring at me. When he took his shoes, and pants off along with his boxers, my pussy pushed my feelings to the side and took over. Raheem's dick was big and thick even when it was soft. Maybe that's what my problem was, I was just horny.

"You were right about shit slowing down for us. The boys are cracking down on watching us and waiting for us to slip up. Tonight, my boss closed the whole operation for a minute. Until the boys in blue fall back and get off our asses." He said as he went into the bathroom.

I heard him cut the shower on and I got annoyed. I jinxed his ass and now it looks like my income is going to have to carry us. I wouldn't care if I had planned on being with Raheem for good. He still had his controlling ass ways and his rules. I couldn't stay with a person like that. Part of me wanted to walk away and the other part wanted to change him. Raheem had never struck me with his hands. He's only grabbed me rough and made threats. Maybe if we just have a talk and I tell him how I feel we would be good. Raheem came out the bathroom with a towel around his neck and his body wet. I watched him dry off and put deodorant on and take his earrings off.

"So, what are you gonna do now? You know I got you, but I know you are not about to just sit in the house." I said to him as he climbed in bed and turned the TV on.

"Hell naw! I ain't no damn house wife. Me, Smoke and Eddie were talking about doing a lick. Eddie was thinking of hitting this warehouse up. His cousin used to cut, and pack dope up there. He told us it's real money all up and through there. If we hit that shit up, we getting out of Miami. That's some real money and I ain't tryna have whoever runs that muthafucka on my back. I told him we ain't doing shit until we find out more about who running that muthafucka. Pick a state for us because we will be done with Florida." I sat up because the shit Raheem was saying was crazy. No way was I going to leave Miami and go on the run with him. I needed to be careful with how I chose my next words.

"Raheem boo, I really want you to think about this. A lot of robberies go bad and I don't want anything to ever happen to you boo. That would fuck me up." I looked at him. He studied me like he was trying to figure out if I was full of shit or not. Hell, I wasn't completely lying. I didn't want anything to happen to him. He was no fucking lick hitter and neither were smoke and Eddie. Hell, they barely stole cars right.

"Angel face I would never put myself at risk of never seeing you again. I'm doing this shit the right way. I'm a man first and I am not about to live off of you. Your money you make is fall back money if shit was to get to crazy. But it's my job to make sure that never happens." He pulled me over to him by my t-shirt I had on. He kissed me pulling and sucking on my tongue. I was so horny and ready to relieve some stress. Maybe this dick will put me to sleep and thoughts of you know who will be gone.

"Take this shit off and suck this dick." I pulled my shirt off and did exactly what he said. I was so wet and ready to fuck but my mouth was wet too so some dick in it wouldn't hurt.

I crawled between his legs and looked at his hard-black dick. I licked my lips and took his head in my mouth. I closed my eyes and Brandon's face popped in my head. I was right back at the house party in Miami giving him head in his room. He had my hair in a ponytail in his big hands. I swallowed his dick whole and he moaned my name so sexy. I had slob falling from my mouth on to his balls getting them wet. I could feel Brandon's dick growing inside my mouth. I wanted to gag but I took the shit like a soldier and kept sucking. I was getting so turned on that I started playing with my pussy. I was holding myself up and the other one rubbing on my clit. My jaws had such a grip I didn't need any hands. I more I sucked and rubbed on my clit the more he moaned and called my name. We both came together. His cum slid down my throat smooth like fine wine.

"Shit angel face! I don't know what the fuck that was, but that shit was it! Damn you sucked my dick so fucking good. Come here." I climbed on top of him and kissed him.

Now, I am about to sound like a crazy bitch. But with my eyes open and all, you couldn't tell me I wasn't with Brandon. I don't know what happened to my vision, but Raheem was gone. Brandon was kissing me. Brandon was touching me and making me wet. Even when Raheem spoke. It was Brandy's deep ass voice. I was so ready to feel his dick in me. Still on top, I lifted up and slid down on him. I almost fell over to the side when I felt his thick dick in me. I didn't move at first. I just savored the moment because who the fuck knew when we would do this again. His hands gripped my ass tight and I started moving slow and riding him like my favorite ride at Six Flags. I held his hands down with my hands and bounced my ass like I was on stage.

"Fuck angel face! Tha fuck has gotten into you? You ridin' my dick like you really need a nigga. Do you need me angel face, huh?" Brandon's sexy ass moaned in my ear. I looked down at his gorgeous ass face and said.

"Yesssss boo. I need you so bad ughhh! I need you boooo." I came so hard on his dick. The shit felt so good. I slowed down and you could hear my creamy nut gushing out of me as I slid up and down him. Brandon grabbed my hips and slammed me down a few times and his kids shot all up me.

"GOD DAMN GIRL!" He moaned and started breathing hard. I was kissing on his neck and chest. I got up to clean both of us off. When I climbed back in bed my vision must have cleared up because now I was looking at Raheem. I leaned over and kissed him a few times before getting comfortable under the covers. Raheem put his arms around me and kissed my neck. I cannot believe I just imagined Brandon while fucking my nigga. I felt my eyes get low and soon sleep grabbed my ass. I guess the dick helped, it just was the wrong person's dick.

**

"Girl I'm excited about this performance. It's two bachelor parties going on out there, so you know once we are up we cleanin' up all the money." Sarah laughed and said has she put her duffle bag in her locker. We had just arrived at Legz and it was packed. She was right, we were definitely cleaning up all the bread tonight. I was putting up more and more money without Raheem finding out. I didn't even tell Sarah. Even though she was my best friend, she still was fucking Raheem's best friend. So, to be safe and stop me from beating her ass, I just didn't tell her.

"Well, we got a minute before we go on. I'm going to get a drink and I'll be back." I told Sarah as I walked out the locker room.

You couldn't wear your stage clothes on the floor if you haven't hit the stage yet. Unless you came to only work the floor, you had to be fully covered. I had on some ripped jeans and a black cami with some black and white Puma's. I looked around and saw money, niggas, strippers and bottles being popped. Going to the bar I was happy as hell Tricks and Elicia were working the bar. We got along great ever since my first night so that means my drinks were gonna be good and not watered down. If you worked here your drinks and food were free.

"Hey Tricks boo! Shit live as fuck here tonight!" I yelled over A$AP Rocky Problems song.

"Hey sexy baby! Hell yea, when you and Salt hit the stage have y'all trash bags ready! They gone die when they see the swirl!" She yelled as she put a glass of pineapple Cîroc in front of me. That was my favorite drink and since I haven't been on stage yet. I didn't need anything heavy. She walked away to attend to the many of customers. If I wasn't dancing, I would have worked the bar. The niggas tipped them so damn good. Of course, their looks help but still. Tricks went home with seven-hundred dollars the other night.

"Now, you throwin' that Cîroc back yo' ass bet not throw up on my stage." I turned around and Brandon's fine ass was standing behind me. He looked so good I wanted to jump on him. He was looking so hood but yet you could smell the money on him. He had on a black and white Adidas track suit. It was on his body loose but snug enough to see his sexy ass form. His black and white Adidas high top and black fitted hat he wore made him look like a thug God. Once again, he was iced out with a chain, watch and earrings. This shit was ridiculous to be this fucking good.

"Ain't nobody about to throw up on yo' stage. You forgot I own that muthafucka whenever I'm up there." I smirked and took a sip of my drink through the straw. He smirked back and nodded his head.

"So, why you doing this anyways? I mean don't get me wrong, you're good at it. But the last time we talked you were about to go to school and work on your lash bar." I could not believe he fucking remembered that. What the hell does that mean? Has he been thinking about me this entire time?

"I didn't even think you remembered that." I smiled at him and took another sip of my drink.

"Shit you talked about it the whole damn time at the party, how the hell could I forget? Answer my question." He walked over and stood next to me at the bar.

"Well, I got side tracked with some personal shit with my mama. Then I wanted to stack my money first. I worked at Wendy's and I'm still in school. The lash bar will happen in due time." I shrugged my shoulders and took another sip of my drink. I could feel his eyes on me.

"The way you dance it will be soon enough." I looked up at him and our eyes met. Damn I gotta say it again. Brandon Royal is just simply fucking gorgeous. I broke our stare and focused on my drink.

"Who is Williams? On the tables and chairs the name Williams is engraved on them." I asked just to break the awkwardness.

"That's my last name." He responded tilting his hat to the side.

"Oh, I thought your last name was Royal like your brothers." I looked up at him and said.

"They aren't my blood brothers. We have been friends so long we call each other brother," He said to me with our eyes meeting again. As much as I wanted Brandon, too much is in the way. It's more drama that I don't need.

"Um, I gotta go get ready. Thanks for the talk, you helped time fly by." I smiled at him and headed to the locker room.

Get it together Blair! That nigga is married, and you have a nigga. I said to myself as I walked to the locker room. Sarah was getting dressed. We were wearing matching fish net shirts that stopped right on top of our asses. We were topless under it with just a black G-string under it. With our clear six-inch pumps on we were ready to hit the stage. I was always a little nervous when we were due to perform. I knew we were about to kill it, but I still was nervous. The DJ blacked out the stage with just the white big search light on the pole. Meek Mill feat Chris Brown song Whatever You Want began to play and I got ready to make my entrance with Sarah behind me ready to come on her que.

Girl, as long as you, wrap your arms 'round me

Ooh baby, I don't care what them people say
I'm givin' you whatever you want
Girl, you know I can provide
Whatever you need
Whatever you need, babe
Listen to your heart, baby

I was killing the pole. Those classes were paying off and the tricks Solo taught me, and Sarah made the niggas rain money on the stage. Sarah was out now and together on the same pole we did shit on it as if it was a dick we were sharing. I was now on top of her flickering my tongue in her face and she was biting her lip and making her ass cheeks clap. If you could see the niggas faces as they rained money all over the stage. Sarah got to doing the splits and hip rolling at the same time. I seductively eased out of my fishnet shirt and when I did I noticed Brandon was leaning against the bar watching me. He had his hat low and his dark liquor in his hand. Everybody in the room disappeared and it was just him in the room. I kept my eyes on him the entire time I was dancing. He kept his same expression, but his eyes stayed glued to me and his bottom lip stayed in his mouth.

What makes you think that I would try to run a game
on you?
Just as sure as my name is Dolla, I'll be there for you and I'll
Treat you just like a queen and give you fine things
You'll never have to worry 'bout another in your place, so
believe me when I say

The song ended and me and Sarah raped these niggas' pockets. Just like Tricks said, we needed security to come with trash bags and help us. As we cleaned up I noticed Brandon was not where he was standing at. I hope he didn't leave. I was about to work the floor and was hoping we could talk some more.

"Bitch look at all this money! I'm going shopping tomorrow and you're coming with me." Sarah said. I wasn't going to go but if I didn't spend some money then her and Raheem would be wondering what was I doing with my money. So, I played along.

"Hell yea bitch! Then when we work the floor that's more money." I said as security carried the bags of money to the back. They had to count all your money, take the club cut and we get ours. Me and Sarah went to the locker room to get cleaned and changed. I was going to work the floor but shit, I'm tired and ready to go home. Sarah decided to stay so she was in her other sexy ass attire looking good. I got up to tell Cole I was about to leave.

"Ok baby girl, Brandon has your money in his office. Good show tonight too baby." Cole told me when I walked out the locker room.

Cole and Travis were fine as hell, but they fucked a lot of the dancers here. I was not about to get wrapped up in that damn drama. I started to get nervous when he said Brandon had my money. I thought the money would be in the count room like always. That must mean Brandon wanted to see me. Lord I hope he is not about to chew my head off for staring at him while I danced. Hell, he was looking at me first, so he should kick his own ass. I walked to his office, took a deep breath and tapped on the door. When he gave me the ok to go in I opened the door. Brandon was sitting at his desk with four neatly stacks in front of him.

"Hey, I thought the count room would have my money." I stood at the door and spoke low. I felt like a nervous child going to the principal's office.

"Yea they do, but I wanted to personally give you this. You did your damn thing and earned this four grand."

He got up and walked around his desk. Brandon placed the money in a small bag and held it out to me. I walked towards him and grabbed it out his hand. I gave him a half smile and told him thank you.

"Why you act so scared and nervous around me? I ain't about to do shit to you." He said as he took his hat off. Jesus take the wheel, why did you make this nigga so fine?!

"I'm not it's just you're a little intimidating. You didn't want me here for reasons I understand and now you're acting nice. I don't know how to take that." I honestly told him. He walked closer to me and with the most serious face he said.

"I ain't no threat to you as long as you're not a threat to me." I looked up at him and nervously bit my bottom lip.

"I'm not Brandon." I said low but I'm sure he heard me.

"Good." His sexy voice held on to me so tight. I smiled and placed the small bag on my shoulder.

"Well, thank you again for the congrads and I will see you on my next shift. I have class in the morning." I lied. I just needed to get out his office. I didn't like how I was feeling and Mrs. Kitty was taking over.

"Ok baby girl. Have a good night and don't forget to grab Dino and have him walk you to your car. Even though the parking lot is gated and blacked out you still can never be too careful." He told me. I nodded my head and left out hid office.

When I closed the door, I leaned against it and closed my eyes for a second. Taking a deep breath in and letting it out I looked around for Dino. My eyes landed on Sarah and she smirked at me and winked. I knew she saw when I came out of Brandon's office. I found Dino and he walked me to my car. Driving home all I thought about was Brandon, him watching me dance and his sultry deep voice.

I needed to get home and fuck the shit out of Raheem while thinking about Brandon. Lord help me.

Brandon

"Babe get yo' big ass out the ball pit. You're making all the other kids uncomfortable wit'cho black big ass looking creepy." Tiff was standing over me whispering and laughing in my ear. We were at Chuckie Cheese. It was crowded as hell with kids, birthday parties, all types of chaos around. Ya damn right I was in this ball pit with my squeak. She short as hell and these kids big as fuck. The minute one of these muthafuckas knock her down I'm snappin' off rip. Shit, my baby pretty as hell too. These lil niggas might try to fuck with her all under the balls. Nope! I will snap one of these little kid's necks.

"Tiff, I don't care about how I look. My baby came here to have fun not be run down by all these big ass kids." I said back to her. Some lady walked over with her fat ass son. He was eating a big slice of pizza and was about to step in the ball pit.

"Hell no! Take his ass over to the other pit. He comin' all in here with food and shit, belly hittin' the other kids. Go over there." I pointed and looked at the woman and her kid. All the little kids like Brandy were in this ball pit. They were having a ball and were able to do so without big ass kids jumping in being rough.

"You're so damn rude!" The lady said to me storming off and pulling her son with her. I cracked up and Tiff slapped the back of my head.

"Brandon, that was so wrong. You just hurt that little boy's feelings." She said trying not to laugh. The other parents of the kids in the ball pit with me and Brandy were cracking up.

"I don't give a fuck. He was about to hurt these babies' feelings by getting his huge ass in here. He bigger than the whole damn pit." I know I sound like an ass, but I don't give a fuck. I was Brandy's protector and Cleveland Brown Jr. was not comin' up in here. Brandy was sitting down throwing balls around with her little friend she made. She was a cute little white girl with long blonde hair. She was cracking up when Brandy threw the balls. I got up because I had to go get our food from the counter. All you heard were kids screaming and crying. Parents yelling their kid's names and tickets floating all around. I walked up to the counter and the girls were behind there just standing on their phones.

"Excuse me. My buzzer y'all gave me buzzed. My food should be ready. I had the two large pepperoni pizzas, hot wings and cheese stix." I told the chick with the long black and red hair. She looked up at me like I was God himself.

"Oh, yea let me get your food." She said to me smiling and putting up her phone.

"No, I'll get it since I'm closer to the kitchen." The blonde head chick said while smiling and blushing at me.

"Actually, I'll get it since y'all need to take y'all break anyways." The chick with glasses and freckles said. I laughed to myself because they actually were trippin' over who was going to bring me my food. I stood there trying not to laugh as the glasses chick went to get my food and the other two girls were pissed off.

"Here you go handsome. I threw some extra wings and cheese stix in there as well." She told me.

"Good lookin' baby girl. My wife loves y'all wings." I said to here. Her whole face changed, I winked at her and walked off laughing.

I put our food on the table and set us up to eat. My

phone buzzed and I pulled it out to see who was hitting me up. It was Kalvin, he was telling me that him and Karlos were coming to Miami in two weeks. We had some street business we needed to handle. Shit been smooth as fuck in Miami and we wanted to expand to Baltimore and Philly. We had some niggas in both places that wanted to get down with us. With a big shipment coming in we wanted to talk to our Miami crew and see who we wanted to run Philly and Baltimore. Cole and Travis wanted to stay in Miami with me, so they were a no go. Me, Karlos and Kalvin were going to pick who we thought was ready for so much responsibility. Kalvin always thought more level headed than all of us, so we always needed his Dr. Phil ass when we made decisions.

"You know I had to pry her away from her new best friend she made." Tiff walked to our table laughing. Brandy was crying because she had to leave her little friend to come eat. I picked my squeak up and kissed her pretty cheeks. She stopped crying when she saw the pizza and her My Little Pony cup on the table. I set her up and she started eating. Tiff set down and looked at the food then back up at me.

"You got these little thots giving you free food?" She laughed as she took a sip of her Sprite. I shrugged my shoulders and grabbed a slice of pizza. We were throwing down on this good ass Chuckie Cheese food. This was Brandy's first time coming here and I knew because she had so much fun, Tiff was going to want her 3rd birthday to be here. It was cool with me because that meant I wouldn't have to clean up after a kid party if we have it at our house. Brandy's birthday was the 4th of July and it was already June. I guarantee you before we leave here, Tiff will be reserving her spot.

"Um, excuse me. I apologize for interrupting, it's just when you left the older kids start coming in the ball pit knocking all the babies over. Can you please do whatever you did and get them to leave?" The mother of Brandy's little friend came over to our table and asked me. She was holding her baby who was crying. I got mad as hell. Tiff let the lady sit down and gave her baby some pizza. I wiped my mouth, stood up and went to go get some order in this muthafucka. Chuckie Cheese need to put me on the payroll.

**

"Good night my squeak." I was standing next to Brandy's queen size bed looking down at her pretty self. She was so tired that after her bath she was sleep while I put her pajamas on. I turned her light off and walked out her room. Today was long as hell dealing with all those damn kids at Chuckie Cheese. Just like I said, Tiff made her reservation on the 4th for Brandy's birthday. I didn't want to have to fight kids so I talked to the manager and owner and rented the whole establishment out for five hours. I told them If I wanted the full service, games, food, that annoying ass band that played on the stage. And I wanted the whole place decorated in My Little Pony. I also wanted the number 3 balloons around and a Happy Birthday banner. They were more than happy to oblige when they saw I had money. I'm telling y'all money talks all the damn time!

"She knocked out?" Tiff asked me as I walked in our bedroom. She was putting that apple smelling lotion on her legs. I loved the way that shit smelled on her.

"Yea she tapped out in the middle of me putting her pajamas on." I walked up to Tiff and put my arms around her waist. She smelled so good and skin was so soft. I knew she washed her hair because it smelled like coconut. I kissed her neck and pulled her beater over her head. I don't even know why she had that on anyways. I told her ass I wanted some pussy.

"You smell so good like always. Love making tonight

brown sugar. You cool with that?" I asked her while still kissing her neck. She bit her lip and nodded her head. Tiff knew I hated when she didn't respond. I turned her around and picked her up by her thighs. Her legs wrapped tight around my torso like I liked.

"Open that sexy ass mouth and answer me." I told her as I walked to our king size bed. I laid her down and hovered over her waiting to hear her voice.

"Yes Brandon, I'm cool with making love." Her voice was so sexy and low. I smirked and bent down to kiss her. Tiff wrapped her legs around my neck and swirled her tongue all in my mouth.

My dick was screaming. With our lips still kissing I laid down and pulled her on top of me. I wanted her to ride. Her skin felt so good on mines. She lifted up and put her warm ass pussy on my dick. When she grabbed the rail of the bed I took the liberty of licking and sucking on her chocolate nipples. Tiff was moaning and riding me so good. I had both of my hands on her ass cheeks massaging them with me nails.

"Fuck brown sugar. Pop that warm ass pussy. Shit Tiff." She had me moaning like a fucking bitch. Tiff was licking and biting my neck.

She set up with my dick still in her and she got in squat position. When I looked up at her I don't know what the fuck happened, but I wasn't looking at my wife. I was looking at Blair. Blair was bouncing on my dick like a damn basketball on the court. I was breathing hard as fuck because the shit was feeling good. I kept opening and closing my eyes, so I could get my wife back. Tiff started moaning and her voice was replaced by Blair's voice. The shit was fucking me up so bad. I flipped her over and started fucking her. I refused to look down until I got my shit together. I kissed and sucked on Tiff's neck and tittes. Thinking it was safe to look down I did. And I swear Blair was looking back at me. I closed my eyes and kissed my wife deep. She moaned against my mouth and scratched up my back. when I pulled away and looked at her she still was Blair. I felt like I was losing my fucking mind. I couldn't fuck anymore.

"Stop, stop." I said as I eased out Tiff. I know she was about to kill me for fucking up our nut. All these years we have had sex, I have never stopped in the middle of us gettin' it in.

"What's wrong babe?" Tiff asked breathing hard as she set up behind me. I was sitting on the bed with my head down in my hands. I didn't want to look at her because I was liable to swing if she looked like Blair.

"Babe, look at me." She grabbed my head and turned it to her. I slowly opened my eyes and looked at my wife. Tiff was back looking at me with her pretty ass face.

"What's wrong?" She looked so concerned. I felt bad as fuck thinking about another bitch as I was making love to my wife. Apart of me wanted to tell her what was going on. But then again, wasn't shit going on. Me and Blair wasn't doing anything and never will. I think maybe because I saw her dance that night must have been why she was on my mind. Or it could be because I ain't shit. I lied to my wife about how far I went with this girl. Then I let her work for me knowing I shouldn't have. Looking at Tiff right now, it was no way I could tell her that shit. We have come too far for some old shit to fuck us up.

"I'm good brown sugar. I was getting a charley horse in my fucking thigh." I tried to play it off and make it seem like it was some physical shit that was fucking up my stroke game.

"You ok, do you need to soak in a hot bath. I can make you one real quick." Tiff suggested while kissing on my back and shoulders. My brown sugar was so sweet. I looked at her and kissed her lips a few times.

"Only if you join me." I said to her. She smiled and said ok. Getting up and walking to the bathroom I let out a sigh and fell back on the bed. I needed to get myself together quick as fuck. No way was I ever losing my family over a bitch. I know who I want, and I know I can't let this Blair shit fuck up my home. Man the fuck up Brandon and fix this shit!

The next afternoon

"Yo mama gone kill me for getting you some more toys. But I'll handle mama, ok squeak." I looked at my cute daughter. She was laughing playing with her new baby doll I just brought her. We were at Dolphin Mall and leaving out the Toys R Us Outlet. Tiff had to work today so I decided to take my squeak shopping. My wife is going to kill me about buying Brandy some more toys. Especially because her birthday is a few weeks away. But I didn't care, Tiff know who the fucking boss is.

"Brandon." I heard someone say my name. I was holding Brandy in my arms. Tiff always said she didn't understand why I never took Brandy's stroller. I wasn't about that stroller life. If my squeak got tired of walking, then I would just carry her. Hell, it's what I had arms for. I turned around and saw Blair with the white bitch she dances with. The both were looking good and holding shopping bags.

"What's good wit'chu Blair. What's up Sarah." I said while nodding my head at both of them. Sarah looked shocked that I knew her name. But I knew everybody's full name and personal information who worked for me. My bros pops taught me a long time ago that knowing that shit was good to know.

"Oh, my goodness, is this your daughter?" Blair asked smiling at Brandy. I looked at my pretty daughter and smiled.

"Yea this my squeak right here." Brandy looked at Blair and for the first time I saw her mama all over her face. I had to laugh out loud because the shit was funny.

"Hi little pretty mama." Blair smiled big and looked at Brandy. Brandy threw her doll at Blair and started laughing.

"Oh shit, my fault about that. Her little ass is wild." I said as Blair picked up Brandy's doll. Thank God, she was laughing because I would hate to turn up at the mall if she would have gave my baby a ugly look. Brandy took the doll from Blair still laughing.

"Be nice squeak" I smiled at Brandy. She turned around and laid her head on my shoulder.

"Well we're about to finish shopping. I guess I'll see you at work." Blair said I nodded and told them bye. When they turned to walk away I noticed how fat Blair's ass was in her leggings. I shook my head and went the opposite direction. Brandy was wide awoke laying on my shoulder.

"You yo' mama's child." I laughed and kissed her on the cheek. I need to spend a few bands to take my mind off of this shit.

Blair

"Are you guys ready to place your order?" Our waitress asked as she set I and Raheem's Pepsi on the table. We were at Applebee's getting some lunch. I had to work tonight, and Raheem wanted us to spend the day together. We went to Walmart and got some stuff for the house, then we went to the mall. Now, we both were hungry, and Raheem said he had something he wanted to talk to me about.

"Yea were ready to order. We both want the appetizer sampler platter. He wants the whisky burger well done and I'll have the sirloin stir-fry." She wrote our food down and took both of our orders. Raheem was so busy texting on his phone he didn't even notice the waitress was here.

"Raheem, are you going to stay on the phone our entire lunch date?" I asked getting annoyed.

"Naw, I'm sorry angel face I was handling business. Look though, I need to rap wit'chu about some shit." He told me as he put his phone face down on the table. I looked at his phone and back at him so he can know I noticed it.

"What about?" I responded.

"I found out more information about that lick I told you me, Eddie and Smoke tryna hit." He was wearing a smug look on his face like he was about to deliver some good news.

"It's those Royal Brothers that supposedly run Miami and a whole bunch of other shit. One of them owns the club you dance at. Brandon, I believe his name is. Social media tells all. Anyways, I can tell that nigga not blood cause them other niggas yellow and he black as hell. Angel face I need you to get in good with him and find out some shit about him and their operation." The waiter came and gave us our food. I sat on my side of the booth looking shocked and scared at the same time. My heart dropped, and I felt like I had to throw up. God why are you punishing me? I know I ain't perfect but damn! Why would you put me in this situation?

"Angel face, you good. You look like your about to throw up." I snapped out of my thoughts and quickly pulled myself together.

"Yea I'm straight, just hungry as hell. But boo I don't know about that idea. I mean I don't even talk to my boss. I deal with these two other guys who pays us our money we made after we are done for the night. Even if I could get close to my boss. What makes you think he would spill his business to me. Plus, he's married." I tried to keep my expressions the same so Raheem wouldn't read me or think I'm bullshitting.

"Your right about that. But look at you, even if the nigga is married no nigga can resist you. I'm gone put it to you like this." He leaned closer in my direction and took his toothpick out his mouth.

"I know more about the nigga then you think. I know he got a wife and kid. I know where he lays his head at. I know the nigga is paid out the ass. Either we hit their warehouse up or we hit his crib up. But understand this angel face. Eddie don't like leaving witnesses, so his wife and daughter will get finished." He sat back and started eating his food.

"So, like I said. Get close to that nigga and find out some shit that's beneficial." He said as he continued eating. At that point, I wasn't even hungry anymore. My stomach was in knots and my heart was beating so fast I felt like I needed to stop it from falling out. What the fuck was I going to do now?!

**

Tonight, me and Sarah were not set to perform. But I talked to Cole and he told me I could work the floor if I wanted to. I was learning two things about this business. One, it's an industry that sells sex! There is no way around it or no way to sugar coat it. Two, the girls here will hate on your soul if they feel like you're a threat. And myself and Sarah were considered a threat. We only fucked with each other because the rest of the girls were shady as hell. A few nights ago, we were about to perform and one of Sarah's heels just mysteriously disappeared. We looked everywhere and couldn't find it. Luckily, I had an extra pair and we wore the same size. When we got done with our performance her shoe was sitting in her station. These hoes were begging for an ass whopping.

I was also eager to come to work tonight in hopes of seeing Brandon. He has been pretty distance lately. If he is here he doesn't talk to me and when I do speak he just nods and keeps it moving. I don't know if I did something or if he is going through some shit. Either way I was finding out tonight. If anything, I felt we were becoming friends and were cool. Plus, I really debated if I should tell him about Raheem's plan. I wasn't for anybody dying or getting hurt especially children. Raheem was right about Eddie's crazy ass. He was short a few screws and would kill anybody anywhere. But after me and Raheem's lunch he dropped me off and went to handle some business. I took it upon myself to do some research on my own.

I went on all of Brandon and his brother's social media sites. First off, can we just take a minute and recognize how fine they all are. I just wanna thank their parents for creating such fine ass off springs. Second, their wives were the luckiest bitches on the planet. They took them all over the fucking map. They lived in homes you see celebrities live in. Drive cars that were not even made in the U.S. And their children were beautiful. Sarah was following Karlos wife on Snapchat. That bitch watched her shit like they were short movies. Sarah wanted Karlos so bad and that was the closest she was getting to him. Anyways, based on their lifestyle I was smart enough to learn drugs were not the only thing they were involved in. Don't get me wrong I know when you do the shit right being a drug dealer can pay well. But this was other type of money as well.

So, I decided I was going to lie to Raheem and tell him Brandon and his brothers had their hands in a few dirty dealings. Fake money, weapons and prostitution. Hell, it wasn't like he would know I was lying. All I needed to do was make him think I was getting close to Brandon. I had to make it seem like I got close to him off conversation only. If Raheem thought I was giving up some ass he would flip. I didn't need to be back in the basement for weeks. After Raheem does his lick, I was leaving. I haven't made up my mind yet if I was going to stay in Miami or not. All's I know is I needed to get away from Raheem. I felt bad that he was hittin' up Brandon and his brother's spot. But I'd rather it be that than his wife and child. Even though I wanted her husband doesn't mean I wanted Tiff and their daughter to die. Doing things this way would secure my safety, Brandon's and his family. And Brandon and my friendship would not be fucked up.

"Bitch stop will you stop watching that girl's Snap videos?" I yelled at Sarah while I was putting on my heels. I was working the floor tonight in my black Calvin Klein thong and matching sports bra. I had the one that snapped in the front so it's easy to take off.

"Girl, I can't help it! Karlos is so fucking fine with them big lips and long hair. I just wish his fucking wife wasn't in the videos." I laughed and shook my head at her stupid ass. I had saw some of Kylee's snaps to. If I had to base their relationship off of those videos. I'd say Sarah had no chance in hell of getting him. I just laughed at her ass and walked out on the floor.

Like always, the crowd was thick as fuck. I looked around to scan the room and saw some potential ballers who I wanted to stay clear from. Those the ones who held on to their money and wanted free dances. I was looking for suits, work uniforms or old ass men whose balls were shriveled up. Those were the ones who spent the money on you. They weren't used to having fine ass women in their faces. I went to the bar to grab a drink first. Alcohol always made me loosen up. My girls weren't working the bar tonight, so I had to deal with these hoes and their nasty attitudes. I wasn't worried about them doing shit to my drink. Thanks to the mirrors everywhere I was able to keep an eye on them.

"Hey Dream, can I have Cîroc pineapple and a bowl of pineapples?" I smiled at the bartender named Dream.

If you ask me the bitch should have been called Nightmare. She had a nice body and face but her attitude was nasty as fuck. But niggas weren't in here for our attitudes so whatever. Dream rolled her eyes and made my drink like it was stressing her fucking life out. I sat there and laughed to myself. While she put my pineapples in a bowl I saw Brandon fine ass walking to his office. He was looking down on his phone. I swear my pussy wanted to follow him through hell and back. He looked like a whole fucking meal in some jean shorts, a sleeveless Ndamukong Suh jersey on with his chocolate built arms showing. I just wanted him to wrap them around my waist and kiss on my neck. His crisp high-top Air Force Ones made his whole outfit complete. Like always, he his risk was on froze along with his ears and neck. Swear he had to have brought out all the diamonds in Florida. Dream put my drink and pineapples in front of me breaking my trance.

"He don't fuck with us on that level, so stop drooling." She said as she walked away. I smacked my lips and rolled my eyes at her.

As much as I wanted to snap on her, there was money that needed to be made. The DJ was playing Chris Brown Strip song as a dancer took to the stage. My mind was on Brandon as I downed my drink faster than usual. I needed some courage because before I hit the floor. I wanted to go talk to him and see what's up. Getting up I fixed my garter around my thigh and walked to his office. I was so nervous that I felt my breathing change. This could go either bad or good. Standing in front of his door I took a deep breath and knocked on it. When he gave me the ok to come in I opened the door slowly and walked in closing it behind me.

"Hi Brandon. I just wanted to come in here and check on you." I asked smiling still leaned against the door. He looked up from his phone and when he saw me his nostrils flared. I had to calm myself down from thinking the worst.

"What do you want Blair?" His expression turned annoyed along with his tone. I had to gather my words because his response threw me off. I cleared my throat and talked.

"It's just that you have been acting like something is bothering you and I just wanted to check on you." I kept my tone low and sweet. He got up and walked around the front of his desk.

"Something is bothering me. You! I'm in here trying to work and you're in here fucking bothering me." Brandon stood there with his arms folded emotionless. My insides felt like he had just shitted on them.

"I-I-I wasn't trying to bother you------"

"But you are Blair. Get out of here trying to check on me like I'm yo' nigga. Get the fuck on the floor and make some money or go home." When his last words left his mouth, my mouth opened a little and I could feel my eyes water. Before I give him the satisfaction of seeing me cry, I left out his office slamming his stupid ass door. I couldn't believe he just talked to me like that. He was so cold and had no emotion what so ever in his voice. I should pop the fuck off on his ass. Looking around and remembering where I was, I quickly snapped out of it. I wasn't about to let Brandon get me out me out of my money-making mode. That seemed to be the only thing in my life doing right by me. Money.

The next morning
RING!
RING!
RING!
I moaned and groaned as my loud ass ringtone went off on my nightstand. The bright light from the window shinned in my face. I hated when Raheem left the blinds open if he woke up before me. I felt like he did the shit on purpose. I must have been sleeping hard as fuck if I didn't hear him leave. I'm usually a light sleeper unless I had some hard liquor, good weed or some good dick. And last night, I had all of the above. I reached over and grabbed my phone. I saw it was Ester, my mama's neighbor. She probably was calling me to tell me my mother cussed her out again. I was so happy Ester could hold her own against my mama, but I didn't need her driving Ester away. She helped me out a lot by checking up on my mama because it meant I didn't have to do it.

"Good morning Mrs. Ester, how are you?" I talked into the phone.

She spoke back and told me what I thought. My mama had cussed her out about always coming over. We laughed about it and Ester told me that she told my mama to suck a dick. I swear I loved Ester because she took no shit. Then she told me my mother had no food in the house and needed some. The last time I tried to get her some food we fell out and I stormed out and left her ass hungry. Me being me I couldn't leave her like that too long. I told Ester I would stop but when I get dressed and bring some food. I asked her if she needed anything. She told me to get her some Hennessey, eggs and three Swisher sweets. What the hell kind of list is that!? But that was Ester for ya! I told her ok and I would see her in about two hours. I got up, showered, threw on a maxi dress and flip flops and headed out the door.

When I turned down the street to my mama's apartment I saw a car that looked like Raheem's blue Challenger parked outside. In fact, it was his because his custom work he had done on the doors were on it. Confusion was all over my face because what the fuck could he even be doing here. To be safe, I parked around the back of the building, so he couldn't see my car. I grabbed my phone and purse. Unlocking my phone, I checked it to see if he had hit me up. All I had was a be back soon text from him and that's it. I normally would respond but right now I was on some other shit. Why would he be here? I walked to the front of the complex past the leasing office.

I didn't need Chuck seeing me and calling my name. I wanted to stay discreet about me being here. My mother's door was on the second floor behind the leasing office. When I saw it open I ducked in the maintenance door arch way, so I couldn't be seen. Raheem walked out looking pissed off and shaking his head. When he got downstairs closer to where I was hiding I prayed he didn't see me. I could smell his Armani Stronger Than you cologne. That's how close he was to me when he walked past. The brick wall was hiding me, but I still sucked in my stomach just in case. I prayed nobody was in this maintenance door because if they opened it, I was falling straight on my ass. I didn't move until I heard Raheem car start up. He had a special engine in his Challenger so when he started it up it was loud. When I heard him pull off fast I moved from where I was hiding. All kinds of thoughts were going through my mind. Like, was Raheem fucking my mama?

Shit, my daddy touched on me my whole life until he died so I didn't put nothing past nobody. He only had met her once and he didn't even say much to her. What the fuck about my sick ass mama would make him want to stick his dick in her. I mean she was a beautiful woman, but her head was all fucked up and she was sick. Raheem is a sick ass twisted nigga if he was fucking my mama. I walked up the stairs to her door. I stuck my key in slowly because I didn't want her to know I was coming in.

When I walked in the living room TV was on and there was a blanket on the couch. I saw a plate with some pie crust sitting on the table, so I knew Ester must have made her apple pie. Walking to my mama's room slowly I was so nervous on what I was about to see. When I stepped in the room my mama was sitting up in her bed with belt around her arm and a needle in her hand. She was about to shoot up. My eyes got big as saucers and I rushed to her knocking the needle out her hand.

"WHAT THE FUCK ARE YOU DOING?" I yelled at her. She darted her head up in shock and started screaming.

"WHAT THE FUCK ARE YOU DOING IN MY HOUSE!? Get the fuck out Blair I ain't in the mood to see your face today." She got up to get the needle, but I stood in front of it.

"Ma, what the hell is all of this? Why are you using again? And why was Raheem here? Are you fucking him in exchange for drugs?" I asked raising my voice with each question. My mama sat back down and looked up at me and all I saw was hatred in her eyes.

"Girl shut the fuck up! I don't want that young faggot. That's who you been fuckin' all along girl. A fucking faggot!" She said to me while smirking. I stood there and shook my head at her silly lie.

"Ma, Raheem is not a fa-----"

"You so fucking stupid. That nigga is a dick in the booty ass faggot. Caught him kissing Delmar by his car one night." She started coughing but still smiling like the shit was good news. I felt like someone kicked me in my stomach.

"Who is Delmar?" I asked still keeping eye contact with her. My breathing was trying to change on me. Before I panicked I needed to know what she knew.

"He lives downstairs in apartment 3A. He a fine lil' young thang with dreads." She started laughing and clapping her hands.

"This is a senior apartment how-------"

"Girl bye." She waved her hand at me. "Chuck don't give a fuck who he rent to. As long as you got money, he givin' you a key. I told yo' faggot boyfriend that I saw him that night. He begged me not to tell you. The confused nigga really loves you, but he loves dick more. Anyways, I told him if he keeps me supplied then I'd keep his secret. He told me he wasn't a drug dealer, he stole cars. I told his ass every criminal knows other criminals." She started back up laughing hard as fuck. I'm talking Kevin Hart laughing. My tears were coming down like a speed racer. I could not believe what my mama was saying.

"Ma, I'm your daughter, you carried me. How could you be ok with doing me this----"

"BITCH FUCK YOU! IT'S YOU FAULT YOUR FATHER IS GONE AND I'M ALONE! ALL HE WANTED TO DO WAS LOVE YOU LIKE A FATHER------"

"HE WAS A SICK ASS PERVERT WHO FINGER

FUCKED HIS DAUGHTER FROM THE AGE OF FIVE YEARS OLD! I'M GLAD THAT NIGGA BLEW HIS BRAINS OUT!" I shouted. She tried to come at me with a swing, but I moved making her fall on the floor. Mama started coughing hard. I stood there looking down at her with a face full of tears. I walked over to the needle and picked it up. I picked up the belt that was on the floor to. I put both the items on the floor in front of her face. I bent down and lifted her head up, so she could look me in my eyes.

"I hope you overdose and rot in hell just like that sick fuck." I spit in her face and let her hit the floor.

Turning around and walking out I wiped my face. I never planned on seeing that sick ass bitch again. When I opened her door, I saw the apartment in 3A open. Sure enough a young fine light skin guy with dreads walked out. He was talking on his phone, so he didn't pay any attention to me. I almost threw up in my mouth. I walked downstairs feeling like I was in a nightmare. Why the fuck was all of this happening to me? Raheem was a fucking faggot, my mama didn't give a fuck about me. And Brandon treated me like he was my pimp and I was his hoe. When I got to my car I pulled my phone out. I googled clinics near me and put my car in drive. I could cry later once I get tested. My next phone call was to Chuck. He had properties all over Miami and I needed to rent one from him. I was never stepping foot back in the house me and Raheem shared again. Fuck this shit!

Tiff

"And breathe in deep. And out slowly, arms down and head slowly down." I talked in my low soothing voice. I had sounds of the rainforest playing in my surround sound speakers.

"Ok guys, that was a good session today. I will see you all Thursday." I said to my yoga class. This session was very soothing even for myself. I have been needing some relaxation since my home life was tangled up. I don't know what was going on with Brandon, but we had not had sex in two weeks. That may not seem long to anyone with a dry sex life. But me and my babe only went days without fucking if I was on my period. And even then, I would at least suck his dick to get him through the five days of me bleeding. But it's been none of that either. All we do is work, talk here and there and spend time with Brandy. He also has been going to that club a lot lately. We agreed to get him some help running the club so it wouldn't consume all of his time. I don't know what was going on. But you can best believe I will be getting to the bottom if it.

"Excuse me, Mrs. Sexy Yoga instructor." I was on my knees rolling my mat up when I heard a deep voice grab me like I owed it money. Looking up to Quan fine ass face I responded.

"It's Tiff or Mrs. Williams if you must be modest." I told him as I put my mat in the corner. I was trying to get up and he rushed and helped me up. My hands went over his chocolate bicep as he pulled me up. I hurried and let him go and breaking my eye contact.

"Well Tiff it is. I'm Quan if you wanna be modest. Or Smoke if you're not trying to be. You teach a good class, very natural with it. I can tell you been into yoga for a long time. After I left the army I took up yoga to relax my body and mind from all the fucked-up shit I saw." I smiled when he said how yoga helped him after leaving the army. So many of them see things I probably couldn't imagine. That's how a lot of them get PTSD and become messed up. I was glad he found an outlet to help him.

"That's really good Quan. I'm happy you were able to get some peace after going through all of that. Thank you for serving by the way. My father served as well before he started bodybuilding competitions." I told him with pride. He licked his lips and smiled as I talked.

"Oh I have found good peace in your class. You're a fucking dream to watch and your voice is soothing as hell." I blushed and cleared my throat. Enough of this shit, I needed to let him know that I was married before this conversation went any further. He was fine as fuck but he wasn't worth my marriage. Plus, Brandon looked better.

"Before you hit me with the I'm married speech I already know your locked down. Shit, you can see that rock on your finger from the damn moon. I was just telling you how helpful your class is and that you are beautiful as hell." He said while biting his bottom lip.

"Am I interrupting some shit?" I jumped when I heard Brandon's voice enter the room. He was walking in the room towards us with some roses in his hand. I turned in his directions with my hands in the back of my hips. Quan turned too but his smirk was wiped of his face now.

"Hey babe. What are you doing here?" I asked him smiling and trying to ease the tension. Brandon was in my face, but he had his eyes locked on Quan.

"I came to surprise my wife. Who the fuck are you?" He asked with nostrils flared and killing Quan with his death stare. I didn't want anything to go down, so I spoke up.

"Babe, this is Quan. He rents the space in the

basement for boxing lessons. He also is in my yoga class I teach." Keeping my smile, I stepped in front of Brandon and put my hand on his chest. He didn't even budge with his stare at Quan.

"The class over, so why the fuck you still here? Tiff shut the fuck up, I ain't talking to you." He said to me still looking at Quan. I zipped my fucking mouth and just prayed this didn't turn up quick.

"Listen, I meant no disrespect. I was just telling her how her class was helping me." Quan held his hands up in defense as he turned and walked out the room. Brandon looked at me like he was ready to body slam me.

"Why the fuck was he in here talking to you all close in yo' face and shit?" I stepped back and looked at him with that how dare you look.

"Brandon, don't bring yo' ass in here trippin' off shit that is smaller than what'chu making it. He told the truth. He was telling me about him being in the army and yoga helped him when he came home. You the one who been acting funny for the past few weeks. So, kick rocks with yo' nasty ass attitude." I picked up my towel and walked away from his ass. I saw Brandy at the front desk with Laura playing with her toys. I went to kiss and hug my baby. Out the blue Brandon grabbed my ass up in the air and walked to my office.

"Babe what are you doing!" I asked him looking at Laura. She started laughing and shaking her head. We got to my office and he closed and locked my door with me still in his arm. He put me down and pulled me to him kissing me deep and hard as fuck. The shit took my breath away and made my pussy wake all the way up. I pulled away and looked at his sexy ass face.

"Brandon, I need to shower." I said as he broke the front snaps of my sports bra. The buttons hit the floor.

Without saying anything he started sucking and

licking in my nipples so good I almost came from that alone. He used both his big hands to dig inside my shorts and grab my ass cheeks so hard. With his nails digging in me and his wet mouth pulling and licking on my nipples. I came all in my panties. He didn't stop, he put hickey on my neck and titties. He worked his way down to my thighs. He was biting harder than some girls would like but not my ass. I loved a little pain during sex. When he got to my pussy he put one leg over his shoulder and dived in. I was still standing up against the door. Brandon was attacking my clit like it did him wrong his whole life. I had my hand on top of his head pressing his head into my pussy hard as fuck. We were weird like that, but I loved it.

"Holy fuck babe! I can't take it babe my knees are getting weakkkk." I felt my shit giving out and without stopping he slammed me against the door and put my other leg on his shoulder. My body was completely in the air as Brandon's tongue and lips devoured my pussy. I felt like I was on a big ass ecstasy cloud and I never wanted to touch the ground.

"B-B-Brandon shitttttt I'm fucking cummin'! Aw SHIT!" I came so hard I felt like I was being whisked away. Opening my eyes, I realized I was. Brandon still had me in the air walking me to my desk. He laid me down on my back. Looking me in my eyes and biting his lip he pulled his basketball shorts down and took his shirt off. His dick was so hard, and he had precum coming out of it. I was so happy I was on the shot because me and Brandon never used condoms. I loved Brandy with all my heart, but I wanted her to be at least three before I got pregnant again. Brandon sild his dick slowly in me making my back jump. He looked down at my pussy and started rubbing my clit in circles nice and slow. My fucking body was blazin'!

"Shit shit shit Tiff! Yo' pussy so muthafuckin' good. Shit!" I loved hearing Brandon moan like that. It turned me on knowing how good my pussy felt to him. He leaned down and kissed me so good I fell in love all over again. Soon enough we were cummin' together and it felt so fucking great.

"I love you so much brown sugar, no matter what I love you and only you." He kissed me deep taking my words away. Out of all the kisses he has ever given me, this one scared the hell out of me.

Brandon

"Y'all niggas gone catch Tiff's mouth for bringing Brandy all these toys." I told Karlos and Kalvin as they walked in the house. We had some business to attend at the two of them came so we could handle shit real quick.

"Aye nigga, blame the girls for all this shit. I told them we would all be here for Brandy's birthday. Kylee told my ass I couldn't touch her if I didn't bring her niece this shit. So, here you go nigga." Karlos said sitting all the bags on the floor.

"Yea Keira threatened me too with no pussy so shut yo' ass up and let my niece enjoy. They told us these are not birthday toys so let her have them now." Kalvin said as he brought this big ass doll house box in the house. I fell out laughing.

"Man, y'all gotta take control of y'all wives. Get yo' balls back." I told them as I grabbed my shit and laughed.

"Fuck you nigga, I ain't about to not be able to touch my wife. If I had to rent a UHAUL and haul this shit here I would have." Karlos crazy ass laughed as we greeted each other. We walked in my man cave. I had Tiff order us some pizza and wings and a case of Pepsi.

"Hell yea bro I was hungry as fuck! Baby sis always looking out." Kalvin said while his greedy ass grabbed some chicken. We fixed our plates, set down in my movie style chairs with the TV on ESPN.

"So look, our shipment comes soon and we gone have Travis and Cole set the other warehouse up with the new crew. This will give us a chance to see if they can handle this much responsibility. One mistake and they ass is done." Karlos said to me and Kalvin. And just so y'all know, done does not mean they are fired. Those who been reading about this crazy ass nigga knows what "done" means.

"Agreed." Kalvin said while eating some pizza.

"Agreed to. Andre and Blu knows to bring the shipment to our old warehouse. Cole and Travis know to pick it up and take it to the new spot. The new crew we gave them are all set up with packing and getting the shit out. I already told them not to fuck up." I told Karlos and Kalvin. They nodded their heads. We continued to eat, watch ESPN and talk about stupid shit. They were coming to the club with me tomorrow night. I had to work tonight but Karlos and Kalvin were going to the new warehouse with Travis and Cole to check shit out.

"Brandon, we gone!" Tiff yelled to me. I heard the front door open and close. I just shook my head. I wanted to jump up and dig in Tiff's ass but I was going to let it go for now. Believe me she was gone hear me when she got back.

"What the fuck was that?" Kalvin asked as he got up to throw his paper plate away.

"Man she been trippin'." I finished off my Pepsi. I hope my bros don't start digging because I didn't even want to talk about this shit. But then I forgot who was here. Kalvin's ol' Dr. Phil ass.

"Nigga, what the fuck did you do to my baby sister?" Karlos ol' Mufasa voice havin' ass said. I just dropped my head and ran my hand over my fade. I honestly don't know what Tiff problem was. Even after I dicked her ass down in her office she insisted some shit was up with me. Then this Blair shit is fucking with me and I don't know why. I figured fuck it, I gotta talk about this shit before I go crazy. I trusted my bros more than I trusted anybody next to Tiff.

"Y'all remember a few years back when I fucked up and cheated on Tiff when we had that party here?" The both of them said yea.

"Damn bro, I know you didn't cheat again." Kalvin asked.

"Naw nothing like that. I lied to Tiff about what really went down between me and ol'girl. I told her she just sucked my dick. She did but the next day I met up with her and smashed." I put my head down with my hands-on top of my head.

"Ok, I'm lost. Why is this old shit even coming up? You just wanted to come clean?" Karlos asked me. I let out a long breath.

"No, Travis and Cole were hiring dancers and Blair showed up and they hired her. She was the black girl who danced with the white bitch at our grand-opening." I said to them.

"Damn bro." Karlos and Kalvin said in unison.

"Why you didn't fire that bitch. Keep her ass far away and tell that bitch to stay in her lane. Miami belongs to us, so you know how to make her keep her distance. You know what, let me holla at her." Karlos crazy ass said. Even though I wanted this shit to go away I wasn't about to put Killz crazy ass on her.

"Bro, no you don't need to. I already talked to her ass and told her not to cause no trouble. She been working there for about two months and shit been smooth. I was going to fire her the night of the grand-opening but." I stopped and ran my hand across my face.

"But what bro? What, she blackmailing you or some shit?" Karlos asked getting mad. Swear this nigga popped off quicker than a top on a bottle.

"Hell naw she not, I know that look. You feelin' this chick ain't you?" I couldn't even answer. I just put my hand on my face.

"Damn nigga, was the pussy that good?" Karlos asked looking at me with anger. I knew him and Kalvin were mad at my ass. But shit to be fare I haven't done shit.

"Y'all I swear I have not done shit with Blair and I don't want to. I just can't shake her from my brain. She cool as fuck, got good convo and y'all already know how she look." I sounded like a jack ass, but I was being honest.

"Brandon, don't fuck around with fire. I did that shit last year and remember how Keira left my ass. On some real shit, Tiff might not come back my nigga. You right, that bitch is bad as fuck and tempting. But think with yo' big head. That bitch ain't worth losing everything over." Kalvin said to me. Sometimes I couldn't stand this nigga because he made so much sense.

"Fuck that bitch bro. Fire that hoe and I bet all my bread she won't say shit. I wish a muthafucka would try to come between me and Kylee's shit. Even though that bitch is fine and that dancing shit hot as fuck. In my prime, I would-----" Just as Karlos was talking his phone started ringing J. Holiday Suffocate. This yellow nigga looked nervous as fuck. Me and Kalvin laughed because he never looked nervous.

"Baby sis got yo' ass bugged. Her spidey senses get the tingling when you even think of another bitch" Kalvin said cracking up. I fell out laughing at this stupid ass nigga. The shit was weird as fuck that Kylee would call right when Karlos was tellin' us how bad a bitch was. I wouldn't put shit pass them two if she did have his ass bugged.

"Fuck y'all! You good baby." He answered his phone cheesing hard as fuck like a high school bitch. Shit was funny as hell to see how Kylee had him but I couldn't be happier for my bro.

"Aye man, no joke. Don't fuck Tiff over bro. We ain't accepting that bitch if you do decide to fuck with her." Kalvin told me sounding like a joke, but I know he was dead ass. My baby sisters would fuck Blair up on sight every time they would see her.

"You right bro, swear I'm fixing this shit." I meant it

to. Tiff meant everything to me and I couldn't lose her.
　　**

Why, we ain't friends no more? (Why?)
Why you won't listen no more? (Listen)
Damn, I let a good girl go
Away, away, away, I've been
All around the world and I've been lookin' for you, searching
(I've been lookin')
You deserve it 'cause you're perfect

Dave East and Chris Brown Perfect song was playing loud over the club. I was on full display tonight since Cole and Travis were not here. Security was all over making sure shit was tight. The bar was stocked, and the bartenders were all here serving up drinks. Some Spanish chick was on stage getting money rained on her. I was feeling the turn out tonight. We had three birthday parties and VIP was full. I definitely was bringing in some dough tonight. I decided to make bitches pussy leak tonight with what I had on. I wore all black tonight with my jewelry being the only thing that shined on me. I was sipping on some henny feeling real good. I planned on going home and making sweet love to Tiff tonight. It was past due, part of me wants to tell her what's been going on but I'm battling with that choice. I can't lose my brown sugar. She ain't the type to keep me away from my daughter. But I want her too. Blair ain't even worth all the hell that will rain down on me if I was to fuck with her. The lights lowered and Usher Nice and Slow song came on. That white bitch came down the pole with Blair right behind her.

Fuck me! I didn't know she was dancing tonight. I would have taken my black ass to my office. Now, I was stuck stupid looking at her once again dance. I have been watching strippers since I was ten. When I used to sneak with my homie on the block and watch them on pornos. I have seen bitches do tricks on poles and clap they asses like at stadium filled. But, it was something about the way Blair moved on the stage that had a nigga stuck. That's why her ass made so much money each time she stepped in this muthafucka. I watched her while sippin' on my henny wind her hips, shake her ass and fuck the shit out of the pole. Her body was fuckin' killin' and her face matched. I drunk the last of my drink and walked to my office. I was annoyed that I stood there and watched that long.

I walked in my office and set my glass on the end table next to the couch. I alerted security that I was off the floor so watch my fucking spot. I grabbed the remote to the TV and plopped down on the couch. Turning the TV on How To Get Away With Murder TV show I took my fitted off my head and sat it on the couch. This was me and Tiff's favorite show and I was a season behind. Tiff would kill me if I watched this without her, but one episode wasn't gone hurt. I grabbed my phone and decided to text Tiff that I love her. After about ten minutes I looked at my iPhone 8 Plus and saw that she read the text but didn't respond. See, this the shit that's gone make me fuck her up. Now, y'all know I would never hit a woman. After the shit I saw with my grandma that's one thing that I promised to never do. But Tiff ass was pushing me to fuck her up. It's cool though, I'm takin' my frustrations out on that pussy tonight. Sitting here watching TV a knock came to my door.

"It's open." Still sitting on the couch I looked at the door and in walked Blair sexy ass. I looked at my phone and saw the club was closing.

"What can I do for you?" I asked her. She twisted her fingers in her hand as she leaned on the closed door. I stood up and walked around the couch. Whatever she wanted to tell me was making her nervous.

"Blair, what's-----"

"Why do you watch me dance?" She blurted out shocking the fuck out of me. I stood there and looked at her.

"You stop talking to me, then your rude as fuck to me the last time I was in your office. But every time I dance your right there watching me. What's that about?" She finally looked up from her fingers and looked at me.

"To be honest wit'chu Blair you a bad bitch and I'm a nigga with a dick. Why the fuck wouldn't I watch you dance in my fuckin' club." She had me fucked upcoming in my office questioning me. Yea I watched her because she sexy and kills the shit, but I don't watch on no creep shit. My dick doesn't get hard or anything. She smacked her lips and turned to leave. Shit! I wasn't trying to hurt her feelings. I grabbed her hand arm.

"Look, my bad baby girl. I don't mean to be rude it's just I don't do too well with people questioning me. My fault for disrespecting you that day to. I was wrong and never should have come at you like that. I been going through some personal shit and was in my bag that day." I told her and smiled making her smile.

"It's cool Brandon. I figured some shit was off with you that's why I came in here that day to check on you." When she admitted that I felt like shit. I was mean as fuck to her that day over some shit that I was doing.

"Well, I apologize again for the way I spoke. I won't come at you like that no more. You have my word." She smiled at me and nodded. Her phone went off and she pulled it out looking at it.

"I gotta get going, my Uber is outside. Thanks again for apologizing Brandon and I apologize for questioning you." I nodded and she stepped out my office. Fuck me this shit was about to be hard as fuck. I think I might have to fire her ass.

Blair

"Bitch what's going on with you? We don't hang anymore and when we danced together night before last, you were quiet as fuck! Now, Smoke is saying Raheem is looking for you. Soooo I'm not your best friend no more? When were you going to tell me you left his ass?" I looked at Sarah as I put my heels on. She said all that shit in one breath when she came in here slamming her bag on the bench in my face. Clearly, she had some shit to get off her chest and I guess that was it.

"Well damn Sarah, hi to you to." I smiled at her, but she was not smiling back. I got serious and began talking to my best friend.

"Nothing has been going on with me Sarah. I'm sorry for not telling you what's been going on but I'm just wrapping my mind around shit." As Sarah got dressed I told her about what happened with my mama and Raheem. I told her about Brandon snapping on me then apologizing days later. Then I told her that I left my car at Raheem's house after I went to the clinic to get tested. Which, thank God the results came back negative. I told her how Chuck let me rent one of his houses he owns. I left everything I owned at Raheem's house and was never coming back. When I was done Sarah had tears in her eyes.

"Blair, I'm your best friend. I been there for you since that shit with your awful sperm giver. I would have been there for you through this to." She told me giving me a big hug. I hugged her back and wiped her face.

"I know Sarah, it's just I couldn't risk it. Smoke is Raheem's best friend and he's your man. I just didn't want to put you in the middle of my mess." I told her. We both were at work about to work the floor. Sarah had on a fishnet shirt that stopped on her ass. She had no bra and a thong on looking sexy. I wore some ruffle boy shorts and a fitted fishnet crop top with no bra. We were looking good and ready to make some money.

"I understand where you're coming from. But bitch I wanna see this new house and if it makes you feel better I'll Uber to you so Smoke won't track me. Just send me your address." I smiled at her as we walked out the locker room.

I swear Brandon was smart as fuck for opening a club in Miami. His shit stayed packed! I never worked a shift and didn't go home with less than a grand. I was able to pay for my school and save for my big move. Yea, I decided to leave once Raheem does his lick on Brandon. Smoke was Sarah's man so I'm sure she would tell me when he would do it. Before I left Miami though, I was fucking Brandon. I know I switched up fast as fuck but fuck it. Life had been shitty to me and I had been calling myself doing the right thing. But God still fucked me over. So, I was done fighting my feelings. I wanted Brandon Williams and once I succeeded on fucking him I was going to make him choose. If he didn't choose me, then I was telling his wife everything. I'd be long gone by the time he came looking for me, so I didn't fear shit. I wanted him and I know he wanted me.

"Oh my fucking God!" Sarah shouted over DJ Khaled Do you mind song. She had a huge smile on her face and her eyes glowed. I looked in her direction and saw Brandon, Kalvin and Karlos sitting in VIP. I rolled my eyes because I knew why she was excited. She had been obsessed with Karlos since the party they had three-years ago. She didn't get no play then and she wasn't going to get no play now. Actually, now that I'm really looking at him I can see how he got Sarah acting like a thirsty thot. But then there was Brandon fine ass. He had on these Givenchy jeans that fitted him like all jeans should fit a nigga. Once again, he was in all black with the matching short sleeve Givenchy shit. That fuckin' shirt hugged his chest and arms so good that I was fucking jealous.

"Um bitch snap out of it. If you're nice to me when I fuck Karlos tonight, I'll tell him to talk to Brandon." She laughed and stuck her tongue out at me. When she headed towards them I grabbed her arm. This was my best friend, so I didn't want her to humiliate herself. Plus, I have heard some sick shit about that nigga. I don't want her wrapped up with his crazy ass. I don't see how Kylee fucked with him.

"Sarah don't take yo' ass over there. He ain't what the fuck you want. That nigga kills for fun and he tortures people. You couldn't even get him three-years ago boo. You think the shit we hear about him is all leis? Leave that psycho to his fucking wife." She snatched away from me with an attitude.

"Girl bye. He just needs some of this vanilla pussy and he will forget all about his big booty ass wife. I ain't scared like you boo." She kissed my cheek and walked away to them.

I just shook my head and went to the bar. Sarah was grown and if she wanted to make a fool out of herself then who am I to stand in the way. Hell, if she did get the dick then I was definitely fucking Brandon. I decided to mess with some henny tonight. I took three shots and let the alcohol take over. After eating my pineapples, I was ready to work the floor. The DJ threw it way back with a classic ass shaking song Hot Boyz I need a Hot Girl. I found a table full of these Spanish dudes. They were in their mid-fifty's and dressed in Italian suits. All of them had wedding rings on which mean the money was going to be right. I went over there with my sexy walk and ass poking out more than normal. Them dudes took one look at me and three songs later I walked away with four hundred dollars.

Sweating from all the dancing I went back to the bar. Tricks was working tonight so I sat there laughing and talking to her. I was drinking a bottle of FIJI water and fanning myself with my hand. Out the corner of my eye I saw Brandon walk to his office. He was on the phone and biting his sexy lip. He must have been talking to his wife. Jealousy ran through my body as Sarah rushed over to me looking pissed off.

"Can you believe this nigga dissed me. He said my feet were bigger than his. Then when I tried to give him a lap dance he pulled his gun out on me!" I couldn't help but laugh at Sarah. This bitch was really pissed and looking like she was about to cry.

"I told yo' ass to leave him alone, the nigga nuts. Let's just go make some money." I suggested to her.

"Hell naw! The way Brandon let his brother treat me I'll be dammed if I make him some money tonight. I'm going home." She turned around and stormed off to the locker room. I couldn't believe she let that nigga get in the way of all this easy money. I just laughed and shook my head at her.

It was the end of the night and I had never danced so hard. It was so many birthday parties and dudes in here on vacation. I cleaned up so good that I needed a bag and one of the security guards to go from table to table with me. That's one thing I loved that Brandon did. He made sure his entire staff were taken care of. Security wasn't no joke when it came to our safety. We always got our fair share of the money we made. Even the parking lot for the employees was safe for us to come and go. When my Uber came it parked outside of the gate and a security guard walked me to my Uber.

Some of the girls talked about other club's they danced at. The owners didn't give a fuck about their dancers. When I do move I probably won't dance again because my standards have been set high from the treatment I get here. But then again, this fast money has hooked my ass. Zipping my bag up I walked out the locker room. The night was over, and everything was winding down. I walked out ready to call an Uber when someone called my name. I turned around and it was Brandon's fine ass. His eyes were red and he looked like he was high and drunk. He wasn't wobbly or nothing but his eyes didn't look the same.

"Aye how are you getting home?" He asked me as he turned his fitted hat to the side.

"Um, I'm calling an Uber now. I already know, make sure security leaves with me." I smiled at him. He smiled back and bit his lip.

"Naw, it's late as fuck so I can drop you off. If you're cool with that." I looked at his lips while he talked and I felt my PINK joggers rub against my now swollen clit. God why was he so fucking fine.

"Oh, sure. Thank you so much." I kept my cool as we walked outside together.

He was driving his all black Bentley Coupe. He opened the door for me and I climbed in. My nerves were through the roof. I had butterflies and my heart was beating fast. His seats felt like butter and smelled like his Cartier cologne. He climbed in and took his hat off placing it on the back seat. He told me to put my address in the GPS and we started driving. When he played Al Green Love and Happiness song I laughed.

"What's funny?" He asked me looking from the road to me.

"You. You're such an old head. Al Green, really?" I continued to laugh.

"Naw I ain't no old head. You just don't appreciate good ass music. All you wanna here is that pussy twerking music." He said laughing. I smacked my lips.

"So not true! I love me some TLC, Missy Elliot and

SWV." I told him matter of fact.

"Girl close yo' young ass mouth. You named all new people. Al Green is our parent's music, real music. The Temptations, Stevie Wonder, Smokey Robinson. That's real ass music." He was nodding his head to Al Green's voice. I laughed at how serious he was.

"Yea ok grandpa." I teased. He laughed to and we continued to talk about music. When he turned down my block I got sad because I didn't want to get out.

"Thank you so much Brandon for the ride. I would by a car but I'm saving for something." I told him. He nodded his head slowly.

"No problem. You worked all night tonight and it's after one in the morning. Seems only right to take you home.

I smiled and looked at him. Even with red eyes he still was fine as fuck. We just looked at each other. My eyes kept going from his eyes to his mouth. With us alone and him looking so good I tried my luck. Either he rejects me, or he doesn't. I leaned towards him and when he still just looked at me I kissed his lips. At first, it was just a peck. But then my hand went on his shoulder and his went on the back of my head. Soon enough, our tongues started tangling together and I was sucking on his. Brandon's lips were so soft and his breath smelled like mint. Finally, he pulled away. I didn't want him to snap on me so I took the blame.

"Brandon, I swear I'm so sorry. I won't act any different or start drama I swear. I-------"

"Blair, It's cool man. I kissed you too." He looked up at me and squinted his eyes. I nodded and gave him a half smile. Reaching in the back I grabbed my duffle bag and opened the door. Before getting out I said.

"Thanks for the music lesson grandpa." He laughed and so did I. He waited until I got in the house to pull off. I closed the door and pressed my back against it. Touching the bottom of my lips I smiled. Yea, Brandon Williams was going to be mines.

Brandon

"Ok! Ok! One more picture and I swear I'm done." Tiff said as she fixed Brandy's outfit.

Brandy had on a cute one piece with a tutu attached to it. My Little Pony was on the front of the shirt and the tutu was different colors. Tiff had her hair in ponytails with a heart braid in the middle. My squeak looked so beautiful! She was ready to play but Tiff's ass wanted to snap a million pictures of her. Chuckie Cheese did the damn thing and had My Little Pony everywhere along with her banner and number three balloons everywhere just like I requested. Tiff had some shirts made for me and her. Brandy's pretty ass face was on the front and on the back mines said 'Daddy of the Birthday Girl. Tiff's said 'Mommy of the Birthday Girl. We all looked fly as fuck!

Trump would be mad as fuck if he stepped in this muthafucka. Looking around my bros and their wives were here. My sister's family loved Brandy like she was blood. So Kenny Ricci was here along with his four brothers', his mother and two of his sisters. Tiff invited the little babies who were playing in the ball pit with Brandy when we were here a few weeks ago. That along was a mixture of white and Spanish people. Then you got our sexy black asses all up in here to. All the kids were between the ages of newborn to three-years-old so you heard a lot of crying or happy screams. As long as my squeak was happy than I was all for whatever.

"Tiff let my daughter go play. You got enough pictures already." I told Tiff and laughed at her spoiled ass pouting. She let Brandy go and she took off on her little legs. My squeak was so pretty and chocolate.

"Bro you done set the bar with birthday parties.

This was a good idea to rent this out for a few hours. We took Keion to Chuckie Cheese back home for the first time the other day. Man, I was about to beat some kid's ass for knocking my son down." Kevin told me with wrinkles in his forehead. I set some of the gifts down in the corner with the rest of Brandy's shit load of gifts.

"That's how I was too bro! Like I climbed my big ass in the ball pit with my baby. It was big ass kids trying to get in there knocking kid's down with their fat ass stomachs. I was ready to fight!" I told him laughing and walking back over with the rest of my brothers. Kaylin was holding his baby girl in his arms. It was weird seeing him be a father, but he did the shit so good. Kelly was holding their son.

"She cute as fuck bro. You gone have problems." I told him as he took the bottle out of her little mouth. Kennedy was beautiful and at only three months, you could see her mama in her. I was surprised all the noise was not making them fussy. But the Ricci were a loud as family so they probably were used to it.

"Fuck you nigga. I ain't having no problems out my angel. She not gone wanna fuck with niggas until after I'm dead. You gone have the problems!" He pointed to me as he placed Kennedy in her car seat. She was wide a woke looking around.

"Naw I'm gone be straight nigga! Kalvin ass gone have the problems with Kyra pretty ass. She so sweet and quiet those be the ones." I looked at Kalvin cracking up. I knew he was going to get mad.

"Don't make me beat yo' ass bitch. My daughter gone keep that shit on lock forever. School, family and money! That's all she gone focus on." He said while eating some hot wings. I looked at Karlos and that nigga shot me the finger.

"Leave my princess Kaylee out this dumb ass conversation." He mugged the fuck out of us.

"Naw nigga you got the problems now!" Kevin laughed and pointed behind Karlos. Kaylee was holding a little boys hand. He was one of the kids Tiff invited from our Chuckie Cheese visit.

"Tha fuck. Kylee! Why you lettin' her grab niggas hands?" Karlos walked over to them. Kylee was never fazed at Karlos bullshit. Any other bitch and niggas got scared as fuck at his big angry ass. But she always waved that shit off. We were cracking up.

"I'm so fucking happy I got a son." Kevin's smart ass said. That nigga did have it easier than we did. All he had to do was tell his son to wrap the shit up. Then Kimmora was about due with their other son. Even though Kaylin had a son, he still had a daughter also. Which mean he had to go through the shit with Me, Karlos and Kalvin.

"Nigga you just don't talk! How'bout that!" I told his lucky ass.

The rest of Brandy's party turned out to be so good. Tiff had two characters from My Little Pony come. My squeak and Kaylee started crying looking at them. Me and Karlos wasn't having that shit so we kicked them out. The damn Chuckie Cheese characters made them cry also so they had to get the fuck on as well. I made them cover those creepy ass fuckers up on stage too. Brandy busted her piñata. The kids went crazy and started running the best way they could. Our kids were so little and chubby the shit was so cute. All these kids were going home hyper as fuck! Cotton candy machine, candy bags, cake and ice cream. Yea, it's gone take a horse tranquilizer to get Brandy ass down. She had a ball and wore a smile all damn day which made me feel proud. Every penny was worth spending to make her happy.

"Oh, my goodness it was hard getting her to go to sleep. She was so wired and wanted to play with all her toys. I had to read two stories to her little ass before she finally tapped out." Tiff walked in our bedroom yawning and telling me how putting Brandy to bed was. I shook my head laughing.

"I knew she was going to give you hell. Even after I bathed her she was wide awake. I'm happy she had fun today though. She gone give us trouble tomorrow to with all her cousins being here." I told Tiff.

My bros and sister in-laws were not leaving until the day after tomorrow. Me and Tiff were inside out walk-in closet. I was taking off my shirt just as Tiff got naked and grabbed her long silk robe. Her body was so fucking sexy and toned. Like a fucking model or some shit. Her ass was round and perfectly shaped with a flat ass stomach. Them thighs had that gap that made you see each one jiggle as she walked. Lately, Tiff been cold towards me. I don't know why I expected someone who has been knowing me since sixteen wouldn't notice me acting different. We both were twenty-seven years old. That's eleven years of learning each other and knowing how we are.

She knew me and knew some shit was different. Then to make it so bad, I kissed Blair last night. I don't know how that happened and I know y'all cussing me out. But I swear I love my wife and only want her. Blair was just looking good and the weed and alcohol had taken over my whole body. When we fucked years ago I didn't kiss her our put my mouth on her pussy. Only Tiff got that, I know the shit don't make it no better but I'm just being honest. I'm a nigga who fucked up and I gotta come clean to my wife. Just the thought of her maybe leaving me made my chest tighten. I walked up to her as she tightened her robe and put my arms around her waist. I kissed her neck and breathed in her sweet scent.

"Remember how hard it was for me to get you to fuck with me?" I asked her with my lips to her ear. She smirked and nodded her head.

"Hell yea. It was the end of sophomore year. You and Karlos were throwing some niggas against the locker. I looked at y'all and just shook my head. I was with my boyfriend at the time. Darius Lion, the star quarterback." When she smiled I looked at her with an attitude while still holding her waist.

"Fuck that nigga! He bald, fat and works at the gas station now. Just continue with the story." I was annoyed as fuck with her cheesing and shit over his loser ass. Tiff started laughing.

"Anyways, you looked at me and blew a kiss. I rolled my eyes because you had no chill with doing that in front of my boyfriend." She continued to laugh.

"That's because I didn't give a fuck. You were mine when I first saw your pretty brown ass in that cheerleading uniform. I paid no attention to that lame you were with. What I walk up to you and say?" I asked her with a low tone and I kissed the back of her neck.

"You said, 'So, when we gone tell this nigga that you mine?" She shook her head laughing. I laughed to as I kissed her neck some more. I let her continue telling the story.

"I looked at you like you were crazy! Poor Darius looked at Karlos like he feared for his life. He held my had tight while I cussed yo' ass out. I thought that would have made you step the fuck off----" I interrupted.

"But you were wrong as hell. I told Karlos that I was locking you down. None of us were in the process of having just one woman. But something about you and that skin I had to have. I pushed up on you the whole fucking summer." I told her while kissing her ear and opening her robe. I slowly cupped her titties and played with her nipples. Tiff closed her eyes and bit her lip.

"You did push up on me the whole summer and you pulled Darius out his car when we were at the drive-in.

Yelling about him trying to fuck yo' woman. I wasn't even yours. We had never talked one the phone, texted, went out or anything. You were just nuts." She did a light laugh.

"I wasn't nuts, I just knew what I wanted. After that night what happened next?" I asked her while kissing and licking her neck.

"After that happened you asked me so what's it gone be? I looked at you and put my hand in your hand. We walked off and I never looked back." I was don't talking now. Turning her around I took her robe off and lifted her by her thighs. Tiff's legs wrapped around my torso. I looked at her and kissed her lips.

"I love you brown sugar. Remember that shit, I will always love you no matter what." Kissing her deep I walked her to the bathroom. I turned the shower on while still holding her and stepped in. I fucked Tiff so good in the shower. Then I fucked her life up with this dick three times in our bed. I gotta return to the club the day after tomorrow. I was firing Blair that night and closing that door. Kalvin was right about one thing. The shit is not worth everything I loved. And Tiffany and Brandy were everything I loved plus more.

**

It all falls down

"We checked the new spot out with Travis and Cole. They did good getting the shit ready. Me and Kalvin walked around the whole warehouse. Everybody in that muthafucka was ass naked and the security cameras were all good. The new niggas were on alert and the decoys were all ready to go. I had to give them niggas the ok. They did the shit right as if we did it." Karlos told me. We were in our old warehouse packing up the Escalade with our shipment. This was a drug shipment that needed to be packed, shipped to our buyers and some needed to hit the streets. We used this warehouse for meetings only. Now that the new spot was good then we would use that as a drop off spot form now on.

"That's good new bro. Even though Travis and Cole good peeps this is still a business. We run shit a certain way and niggas know when they get on with us." I responded to him. Karlos nodded his head as we loaded up the trick.

"Aye, we need to do another trip. I was talking to Keira and she was saying a Cruise. That shit sounds nice as fuck." Kalvin said while he duct taped one of the boxes up.

"That shit sounds nice as fuck. Me and Tiff could use a vacation. Speaking of Tiff, I decided to fire Blair." I talked while picking up a box. Kalvin ass smiled along with Karlos.

"Smart move nigga." Karlos said.

"Yea, that shit ain't worth it. I thought about the shit hard and I don't want Blair or any other bitch. I want my wife and only her. I'm thinking of telling Tiff just so we won't have any secrets between us. What y'all think?" I spoke as we loaded the last of the boxes.

Closing the door Karlos hit the back of the window letting Cole and Travis know they can leave. We watched them leave as the cop car sitting outside followed them. Yea, we had police on our pay roll in Miami just like back home. Money spoke no matter where you are. Boss shit! We walked back into the door way of the warehouse about to clean up and head out. Minx and Chica were upstairs of the warehouse. They lived here and kept the place under watch. Them sisters were some bad ass Spanish bitches. Looking at them, you didn't think they were in the game and could shoot. But their pops was a sniper in the Army. They grew up around nothing but Pitbull's and guns. They had been rocking with us for six years now.

"So, you really wanna tell Tiff?" Kalvin asked me. As soon as I was about to answer a black Charger came flying in our warehouse. The muthafucka came crashing through threw the half-closed door and hitting the wall. Seems like shit happened in the blink of an eye because just as we jumped from the crash and pulled our guns out some niggas ran from the back door that was open from the car hitting it. Some niggas in all black with black mask over their faces came in shooting.

POW!

POW!

POW!

POW!

POW!

POW!

The shots kept coming as some came from upstairs. I knew it was Chica and Minx. I fired some shots along with my bros. One nigga ran out the door and two of them hit the floor. Our gangster bitches lit they asses up. We got up once the shooting stopped, and the girls were coming down the stairs.

"FUCK!" Karlos yelled. When I looked behind me Kalvin was lying on the floor with two hits to his chest. How the fuck did we not see this.

"HOLY SHIT!" I yelled as Karlos went to see about our brother.

"Kalvin get yo' ass up bro! FUCK!" I ran to get my car from the front. I felt like I was in a fucking nightmare. Lord, please don't take our brother from us. I know we don't do shit you approve of but please. He has a wife and daughter. I pulled on the side of them and helped Karlos get him in the back. Chica and Minx went after that other nigga that ran. Before we got in me and Karlos rushed over to the niggas that were dead. We both pulled there masks off. My eyes bucked when I recognized the nigga who was pushing up on Tiff in her gym laid dead. The other nigga I didn't know but he was still alive coughing up blood. Karlos grabbed him up, that nigga had that murder face on him.

"Who sent you to die bitch ass nigga?" He asked him through gritted teeth. The nigga coughed up more blood.

"R-R-Rah-eem gone kill ya'll muthafuckas." He said and took his last breath. Karlos shot him in the head and we rushed back to the car. Kalvin was in the back laying down eyes closed but was breathing very low. We seeped off into the night to the hospital.

"Swear to God I'm killing all of Miami if my brother dies." Karlos said with the blackest eyes.

"Shit nigga I'm right there with you. One by one." I said in a calm but scary ass tine. He looked at me and nodded. He told Kalvin to hold on and keep breathing.

We got to Emergency and Karlos picked Kalvin up and yelled for help. Putting Kalvin on a gurney they asked us what happened. Of course, we told them a bullshit story about him being shot standing outside by stray bullets. They rolled him in the back while ripping off his clothes. Me and Karlos had blood all over us especially Karlos. He had hugged Kalvin before they took him off.

"Shit, I gotta call Kylee." He said taking out his phone.

I took mine out to and called Tiff. As soon as I told her what happened she reacted like I knew. Tiff screamed and cried on the phone. They were all together, so I could hear Keira scream and cry in the background. That shit made me and Karlos shed a tear. We didn't want our baby sister to go through this shit. Why the fuck did these bitch ass niggas even do this shit? I know niggas hated but damn! Swear we had secret beef we didn't even know about. Then, this nigga was in Tiff's class. So, he had to know she was my wife. The shit was making my fucking head spin. I just wanted to make sure our brother was straight. Me and Karlos paced the room with blood all over us and eyes filled with rage.

I don't know how much time went by, but I didn't

hear shit until I heard Tiff's voice call out to me. When I turned around I saw her, my bros, my sister in-laws come running in. Tiff hugged me tight and started crying. I shed some tears to. Kylee did the same thing with Karlos. I asked her where were the kids. She told me Kenny and his siblings had them at the house. I told her what happened. She was shocked as fuck when I told her who one of the niggas were.

"I-I don't understand. This was a set up?" She asked me while still crying. I wiped her face and hugged her.

"I don't know Tiff, but I promise I'm getting to the bottom of this shit. Karlos already has one our detectives we pay working on finding out who those niggas were. One got away and Chica and Minx were not able to get him. We got this shit." I told her hugging her. I looked over at Keira crying hard as fuck in Kelly's arms. Tiff and Kylee brought me and Karlos a change of shirts. I walked over to them and sat next to Kelly. I tapped Keira and she looked up at me with a face full of tears. Her eyes were puffy and swollen. But my baby sis still was beautiful.

"I swear baby sis, we are getting all them niggas who did this shit." She nodded her head telling me ok. I hugged her tight and kissed the top of her head. Karlos came over and did the same thing. It had been three hours and the waiting was getting annoying. We were ready to find out about Kalvin. The girls were all around Keira still comforting her. The doors opened from the back and two doctors came in our direction.

"Family of Kalvin Royal." He asked and we all jumped up. We let Keira in front because she was his wife. The doctor's looked confused.

"We are his siblings, and this is his wife." I told them. They nodded and gave us a sympathy smile.

"Hello, I'm Doctor Schmitz and this is my intern Reginald. Mr. Royal was shot twice in the chest. One of the bullets hit a major artery so that was why so much blood was lost. We were able to remove both bullets, but we had to do a blood transfusion. He has type O blood type which is very common here, so we were able to do the transfusion successfully. There are a few more tests I want to run on him when he wakes up. Right now, he is in recovery under heavy medication. He will be out for some hours. You're all very lucky because any closer to his heart then he might not have made it." Him and the other doctor smiled at us and told us we can see him.

All of us breathed a sigh of relief and especially Keira. She hugged all of us and thanked me and Karlos for taking care of him. I don't know why she thanked us, we were family. This is what we fucking do. Keira went back to see him first, that was only right to let her have some alone time. Tiff was hugging me and kissing in me. I knew what she was thinking and of course because of the situation she didn't say it. Kylee was all over Karlos as well which was nothing new. But we both knew what both of our wives were thinking.

Shit, I wish it was me instead of Kalvin in that back room. I just felt like he was the good one out of me and my brothers. It had always been that way since we were little. That's why his mama called him baby cakes. The nigga was always the peace maker. The one who talked sense into any of us who were on edge. He wasn't perfect, but he was the mindful one. He was our brother and if one of us got killed it would fuck all of us up. After some time, Keira came back smiling and telling us we could all come back. He wasn't up yet but I take it she was just happy he would pull through. While everyone walked back I saw the doors from outside open. One of our detectives we paid came in. He was holding a folder and headed towards me. The rest of them were already behind the double doors. I turned around and greeted him.

"What'chu find out?" I asked him. He did a light chuckle and said.

"A lot." And handed me the folder.

I told him his payment was at the usual spot and he left. I opened the folder and seen the two niggas that were dead faces. One nigga name was Eddie Lee Author. His parents were killed in a house fire when he was twelve. All he had was a bitch who stayed in Orlando. It was lights out for her ass. I had his school records and all the little bullshit jobs he had. The way he lived and the cars he owned I knew he was in some illegal shit. It wasn't drugs because we had that down pack. I moved on to the next nigga. Quan Tamir Young A.K.A. Smoke. This bitch ass nigga face I had already put in my head. When I saw him talking to my wife I made it my business to make a mental memory of him. His folder was pretty much the same as the other nigga.

He had two brothers who lived in Jacksonville, Florida. I saw his bullshit jobs to. His record showed that he was under investigation for car theft. Not just any kind of cars either. Foreign cars and car parts. Probably selling them after he steals them. Moving on, I saw where he lived which was right here in Miami. When I saw the name that said Sarah Patterson I looked at her picture. Muthafucka! I said to myself. I looked on and saw he had a bike shop with some nigga named Raheem Carey. The address and information were here on him to. I would bet all my money he was the nigga that ran. What I saw next made my nostrils flare up so big I thought they were going to get stuck that way. Blair was this nigga's bitch. I went to the garbage and threw the folder away. I was so fucking mad I didn't even hear my name being called.

"Brandon! Where the fuck are you going? You're not going to see Kalvin?" Tiff came running up to me. I was so mad it's like I heard her, but I didn't.

"I got some shit to do." I turned and walked away. She tried to grab my arm, but I snatched away and hurried out the door. I could hear her calling me, but I would have to just hear her cuss me out later. I was about to go strangle Blair's ass to death.

Driving in the night I looked in my rear-view mirror and looked at the blood on my back seat. My fucking brother could have died, and it was all my fucking fault. I f I would have been thinking with my fucking brain and not my dick then this would have not happened. I could have lost my wife, daughter and brother all over this bitch. She was dying tonight. No matter what she says, I was killing her. I wanted to kill that bitch with my two bare hands. This bitch played me and had her fucking nigga rob us. My thing is, how the fuck did she even know about our warehouse? Now that much it might not have been her doing because I never shared shit personal with her. But the fact that it was her nigga means she needed to die. I turned down her block and as soon as I got to her house. I hopped out so fast I don't know if I closed my door. I banged like I was the fucking police.

"Bran-----" As soon as she opened the door I had my hands around her neck pushing her inside the house. I slammed her against the wall. This was something I had never done before. I had never put my hands on a woman. But this shit was an exception.

"Bitch are you fucking stupid! You told yo' nigga to try and rob me and my brothers. And before you lie, his two friends are fucking dead. My only question to you is, why the FUCK would you think you would get away with this shit?" I asked her as I squeezed harder. She was trying to scratch my hand, but she was losing to much air. I needed to hear what she had to say so, I let her go and she hit the floor. Blair was coughing and crying.

"Brandon, I swear I had nothing to do with what

Raheem did." She was coughing again and still crying.

"Shut the fuck up lying bitch! My fucking brother almost died!" I stood over her yelling.

"I SWEAR! I had already left his ass when I found out he was cheating on me. That's why I'm here now and I don't have a car anymore. I even changed my number and everything." She looked up at me crying hard. My hand print was around her neck but I didn't give a fuck. This bitch was nothing to me.

"If you lie one more time I swear I will torture yo' ass. Where the fuck is yo' nigga at?" I asked her. She still looked at me crying.

"Brandon, please listen to me. Raheem told me he was going to hit a lick, but I swear I didn't know it was you he was hitting. That was before I left him. I would never set you up. I-I-I love you Brandon. I am in love with you. AHH!" She screamed when I grabbed her by her hair. I wasn't trying to hear this bitch confess her love to me. I had no feelings what so ever for this set up bitch.

"Kill all that noise and tell me where the fuck he is?" I looked at her with cold eyes letting her know I wasn't to be fucked with. Just as she was about to talk the door opened and Tiff walked in. I looked at her and she had the same face expression as I had when I was looking at Blair.

"Tiff, what the fuck are you doing here?" I asked her. She held up her iPhone 8 and waved the tracking page in my face. I let Blair go and walked towards her.

"Tiff, please let me-----" Tiff walked passed me and punched the shit out of Blair. Her nose gushed blood and she hit the floor screaming.

"I knew it! I knew you were fucking somebody, but LOVE! This bitch LOVES you! One of your fucking dancers! How cliché! When did you start fucking her?" Tiff looked at me screaming. I was fucking speechless. This is not how I wanted my wife to find this shit out. I can't believe I was that stupid to not know Tiff ass would find me once I left the hospital. I was so fucking pissed I just left.

"Tiff now is not the time for this shit." I said calm to her. She started laughing at me.

"Oh really, because I think it's the perfect time. You leave the hospital where your brother is shot and recovering to see your side ho! So, again I ask. When. Did. You. Start. Fucking. Her." She asked stepping next to me with each word.

"This is not my side bit-----"

"WHEN!" Tiff screamed loud as fuck. Blair was behind her crying holding her nose. I looked at Tiff and the face she gave me told me my next words had to be the truth. I cleared my throat, looked at my wife and talked.

"This is the same girl who I cheated with. Cole and Travis didn't know when they hired her. I found out at the grand-opening that she worked here. I was going to fire her but-----" Tiff cut me off.

"Wait, wait, wait. You have been fucking her since Miami three years ago?" Tiff asked looking like the devil's wife.

"NO! I was just telling you how I know her. Before my grand-opening, I hadn't seen her since the Miami trip." I was trying not to say more but Tiff wasn't having it.

"So, she fell in love from just sucking your dick? Get'cho stupid ass outta here! How long have you been------"

"I didn't just suck his dick." Blair said while using a blanket on the couch to wipe her nose. She stood up with blood still coming out her nose. I wanted to beat her ass.

"Excuse me." Tiff turned and looked at Blair.

"I said, I didn't just suck his dick three years ago. We went to eat, rented a room and we fucked. It wasn't just a quick hit either. We vibed and he wanted to see me after I sucked his dick at the party." Blair stood there looking me in my eyes.

"He is full of shit, he feels something for me. He took me home the other day and we kissed. He told me not to feel bad because he kissed me back. I am in love with Brandon and he may not love me back, but he feels something for me and he knows it." Blair talked and her eyes stayed on me. Tiff turned from her and looked at me as well. The face my wife had said it all. I had broken her heart in a million pieces. I knew standing right there that I had lost her forever. I could feel it and for the first time since my grandma had died. I felt like I had nothing.

"Tiffany." I said as I walked closer to her. She stepped back and put her hand out. With tears falling from her eyes she kept her eyes on mines.

"I apologize Blair. I shouldn't have hit you. Clearly, I'm the one in the wrong. You see, I didn't know that I was the one in the way of you two building something. But I will tell you this, he is yours now. The fact that you made him feel anything for you means he was never mine to begin with." Tiff said with eyes glued to mine. She turned around to leave but was stopped when the door opened and some nigga with a gun walked in.

"Get the fuck back in. The party is just beginning." He said as he walked in leaving the door opened. Tiff walked backwards with her hands up. I pulled her behind me.

"Raheem, how the fuck did you know where I was?" Blair asked crying again.

"You focused on the wrong shit angel face. I been watching you for a few days now when I followed you from work. So, you love this nigga?" He asked Blair while tilting his head towards me.

"Raheem, please go. I don't love you anymore. I just want to move on and put us behind me." Blair told him. He kept moving his gun from me to her fast. I could tell he was high as fuck and not off weed. That was my advantage to knock his ass out. Tiff looked at me because she knew what I was thinking.

"Leave you alone so you can run off into the sunset with this nigga? I don't fucking think so! You left me without so much a good bye. I would never do you like that. And you!" He pointed his gun back to me.

"You took my FUCKING HEART!" He yelled crying. I looked at him like he was crazy.

Nigga, I didn't take yo' bitch from you. She right there and you can have her ass." I told him with my nose turned up. This nigga was crying real tears. Fucking bitch! I hated that I didn't have my heat with me. I figured I didn't need it to kill Blair. I wanted to kill that bitch with my fucking hands.

"I ain't talking about her nigga! I'm talking about Snake! You muthafuckas KILLED HIM! YOU MUTHAFUCKAS TOOK HIM FROM ME!" He cried hard as fuck. I couldn't help but laugh.

"You a fag ass bitch." I said smirking at him.

"Hell yea, I killed that nigga. He said yo' name before my brother put a bullet in his mouth." I told him smiling big. His eyes got big as fuck.

"FUCK YOU!" He shouted.

POW!

I looked at Tiff hit the ground when he shot her in the stomach. I swear it felt like he shot me to.

PHEW!

PHEW!

Dropping to my knees I looked at Tiff's lifeless body. I couldn't even move or touch her. My mouth was open, and tears were falling on my shirt. I can't believe this fag nigga shot my wife. I pulled Tiff in my arms and broke down. I wrapped her arms around my neck hoping like hell I was in a nightmare and I would wake up with us in

Louisiana. Miami never happened, and we were happy in our house.

"Brown sugar, get up babe. I swear you can't leave me like this. You gotta know I love you and only you. I'm sorry for lying to you, just please come back to me and Brandy. Please, please, please brown sugar." I cried so hard I had snot mixed with tear coming out of me. I didn't give a fuck.

"Brandon. Brandon." I looked up and saw Karlos standing over me. He was looking at me with sad eyes.

"We gotta get her to a hospital." Karlos said to me as he stood next to Blair's dead body. I looked next to her and saw that fag nigga dead as well. Karlos looked behind me at him to. He popped him in the head again. Looking back at me he told me to get up, so we can get Tiff to a hospital. I looked down at her and picked her up bridal style. I walked out slowly just as Blair's white friend walked in. She looked around and was about to scream when Karlos shot her in the head.

"Hated that white hoe." I heard him say behind me while he stepped over her body.

Our cleanup crew pulled up outside. When they saw me carry Tiff out they looked sad and shook their heads. I climbed in Karlos truck in the back seat with Tiff. Looking down at her closed eyes I just held her body and cried. I didn't cry this hard when I lost my grandma. This pain was ten times worst. I don't know what to do without her. I could feel her slipping away from me. It's like the more she was drifting the slower my heart was beating. I didn't know we were at the hospital until Karlos opened the door.

"Come on bro." He said to me with a calm tone. I got out the truck with Tiff still in my arms. Walking to the doors I felt like I was walking to my death. The nurses saw me and rushed to us while calling doctors.

"What happened to her?" The nurse asked me. I

couldn't talk. I just looked at the rip Tiff shirt and start working on her.

"She was shot by an intruder." Karlos answered for me. I walked around them as they wheeled my wife to the back. I heard one of the doctors yell that they were losing her. I felt my knees get weak the minute they went through the double doors. Karlos caught me before I hit the floor.

"She can't go man, she can't fuckin' leave me like this!" I was shouting as he held me back from following her.

"I know bro, I know. She gone make it." Karlos was saying to me while trying to hold me back. I wanted to believe what the fuck he was saying bad as hell. This shit can't be life right now.

Tiff

(A week later)

I opened my eyes to the bright light shining in my face. My vision was blurry as hell and the light was hurting my eyes. As my vision became clear, I could see some machines, a big brown door, a TV with basketball on it. I looked around some more and Brandon was sleep in the chair next to my bed holding my hand. I looked down at his hand in mines and lightly shook it. He jumped up when I did.

"Tiffany, oh my God babe." He jumped up and hugged me tight. It was a little uncomfortable, but I was able to hug him back. We hugged, and I could feel his tears on my shoulder. I cried to. The door opened and the nurse stepped in smiling big as hell.

"Mrs. Williams, glad you're awake honey. Your husband here drove all the staff crazy for seven days." She laughed and looked at me and Brandon.

After checking me out and giving me some ice water. The doctor came in after smiling and greeted me as well. She ran down what happened to me since I was checked in. I was shot in the stomach and the bullet impacted my flesh so hard that when it expanded and contrast by the bullet momentum. That caused some damage to my intestines and caused me to almost bleed out. The bullet was removed but I suffered a seizure during surgery. I had never had a seizure before, but the nurse said it was a reaction my body had. After they talked to me and told me in two days I can leave they left the room. I looked at the bandage wrapped around my stomach. I would forever have a small hole but I didn't care about that. I wanted my life. Brandon was kissing my had and still had tears on his eyes.

"I called your mama and dad. They are on their way up here with Brandy. Everybody else is still here to. There coming up also." He told me as he wiped his face.

"Tiffany, I don't know what you remember------" I cut him off.

"Everything, I remember everything Brandon. I also heard and remember everything you said when I was out of it. You talked to me all the time. I heard you tell me the whole story between you and that girl. From what happened at the party three years ago. You meeting back up with her at IHOP. To ya'll having sex. I heard when you said you didn't kiss her or go down on her. I heard all of it. I know Karlos and Kalvin talked to you. You realized that she ain't shit to you. She ain't worth me or Brandy. Yea, I heard it all Brandon." I wiped the tears falling from my face.

"I accept your apology because I know that your truly sorry. When I heard you tell me all your feelings for the situation. Your feelings towards me and you. How if I don't make it you don't know what you would do." My voice cracked, and my tears fell. He was back crying to.

"I heard you tell me how you couldn't have me die thinking that you were leaving me. That you never even thought about leaving me. I heard all your words and I believe them. I really do." I looked at him and rubbed the side of his face.

"But even though I believe you and heard your words. I still want a divorce Brandon. I need a divorce." I told him as my tears rolled down back to back. He broke down.

"Tiffany, brown sugar. Please don't say that to me. I swear I had no ounce of love for that girl. She fuckin' dead and I could care less. I was firing her before all this shit went down. I p-p-promise Tiffany." He was crying hard. I pulled him in and hugged him tight. We cried together, and

I knew that he knew we were over.

"I will always love you Brandon." I whispered in his ear.

"I will always love you to Tiffany." He and I hugged him tighter. I didn't want my marriage to be over. But the moment Brandon lied to me we were over. The moment he allowed himself to feel for another woman, we were over. As much as I loved Brandon and our life together, I couldn't be with him. I gave him my trust, he gave me his lies.

Epilogue

Tiffany

(Five Months Later)

"Who the hell brought eggnog and no alcohol?" Kimmora walked in the kitchen with her cup. I laughed and shook my head at her.

"Kim, you still breast feeding so you can't have shit in yo' eggnog but the nog!" Kevin shouted from the living room. Kim rolled her eyes. She picked my cup up and smelled it.

"Oh, so I'm the only one who gotta drink mine plain. Ugh!" She smacked her lips and put my cup down. Kevin came in the kitchen and took Kacee out her arms. He was just shy of five months and so cute. He was chocolate with curly hair. Just like Keion, he had Kevin's light grey eyes. His jaws made you want to love on him all day.

"Keira, Kalvin is looking really good. His physical therapy paid off. I know you are so proud." I looked at her and said. She turned around looking at him standing up holding Kyra in the air. He was tickling her making her crack up. Swear they were stuck to each other. It was the cutest.

"Happy doesn't even describe it. I'm so happy I put my faith in God and not what those damn doctors were saying. He did the physical therapy for three months and look how good he's walking. I'm beyond proud of him." She turned back to us with tears in her eyes.

We walked over to her and hugged her. The tears in our eyes were all happy tears. I was so happy God showed his love and healing on Kalvin. Keira would have been a mess without him. Now, Kalvin looks like he never was shot. He moves and walks like he did before. Those damn doctors said he never would walk again. When Kalvin woke up he couldn't feel anything in his legs. The fear we all had was nothing compared to how Kalvin felt. He didn't break in front of us, but Keira told us that he broke down. Nobody could blame him, if you were told you would never be mobile again wouldn't you cry. Anyways, turned out Kalvin had Paramyotonia Congenita. In human words it means his muscles wouldn't relax after they contract due to the dysfunction the bullets did to his nerves. He was paralyzed temporarily for those of you who are still confused. Keira and Kalvin weren't hearing it and put in in physical therapy. Now, five months later he is good as new.

"Thank y'all so much for being there through all of this. I love y'all dearly." Keira said as Kelly wiped the tears from her face. We smiled and told he your welcome. Shit we are family first no matter what.

"Tiff your tree is beautiful. Next year I'm doing silver and gold." Kelly said while taking the cookies out the over.

"Girl I went to three Targets and two Walmart's to find those decorations. I wanted to do green and gold. But Brandy fell in love with that black angel. She thought it was a damn Barbie instead of a tree topper. So, I got it for her and switched my colors to silver and gold like the angel." I said as I shrugged my shoulders. It was five days before Christmas. Like always we had our matching pajama night with cookies, eggnog, good food and our loud silly asses.

"Did Brandy trip about your pajamas?" Kylee asked. I shook my head no.

"You know what, I don't even think she noticed I

wasn't matching her and Brandon. She was so excited when she saw him that she didn't pay attention. That's the good thing about having a young child. They don't understand most things that go on. Me and Brandon have been trying really hard to make this process smooth for her. She asked the other day if daddy had a new room. I almost cried in front of her because I knew what she meant. I told her he does have a new room, but he still will see her whenever she wants. She said ok and went back to playing. She hasn't had any sad moments about him not living with us anymore." I told them.

I was relieved that Brandy didn't understand much of what was going on. Me and her moved back to Louisiana in our old house. Brandon didn't take shit too good and I had to change the locks on his ass. He slept outside in his car four nights straight. He parked outside of the house, everyday he tried to come in. He left the club to be managed under Cole and Travis and moved back here as well. After I told him to stop sleeping outside of the house because it wasn't going to change anything. He went and bought a condo. A few weeks after, I had a sit down with him. Just me and him, no lawyers, no kids around. I explained to him that Brandy was the only thing that mattered. We needed to be good parents for her and stop all the drama. He agreed and since October things have been really good. He gets her on the weekends and whenever I got to work.

In November I opened up a yoga studio. I absolutely loved it and couldn't be happier with my new baby. Me and Karlos decided to let Laura manage the gym in Miami. Miami stopped being a home for me when I woke up in the hospital. I never told my mama about the details of me getting shot. All they know is I was at the wrong place at the wrong time and the people who shot me were long gone. When Brandon stormed out the hospital that day I knew some shit was up. I tracked his phone and saw where he was headed. I told my brothers and sisters that I was stepping out for a minute. I lied and said Brandon went home to lay down. They all believed me but Karlos. He told me when I woke up from getting shot that he knew some shit was off. He said no way would we just leave the hospital without seeing Kalvin. I guess I'm happy my big brother did see past the bullshit. If he wasn't there that gay nigga would have killed Brandon and who knows who else.

My parents were so relieved that I was ok and moving back they really don't talk about the details of me getting shot. My recovery was fine, I had to eat liquids for a few weeks and take breathing exercises. But other than that, I was blessed. The hardest thing about all of this was being without Brandon. I missed him so much that sometimes I didn't even sleep at night. I wanted his touch and his love all over me. But, I couldn't get past how he lied and let shit get so out of hand. My heart and mind were battling every fucking day on this. My mind was like fuck him, go get another one. My heart was like bitch bye! You can get another nigga, this much is true. But he won't be no Brandon DeAndre Williams. We still had not served each other divorce papers. I had an attorney and everything. I guess I just haven't gotten to that point.

"Well that's good Tiff. I love how y'all came together and got it together for my niece. I'm proud of y'all." Kylee said as we walked in the living room.

We were about to play some games like we always did when were all spent the night together. Brandy was sitting in Brandon's lap eating a Christmas cookie. I smiled at her and kissed her cheek. I sat down next to them and ignored the fact that Brandon was looking so good in his red and green Christmas pajamas. Him and Brandy matched with the shirts saying, 'Naughty or Nice'. The looked really cute. I wore a onesie with Will Ferrell on it when he was in the movie Elf. Kelly got up with her iPhone 8 ready for us to play charades.

"I can't believe we messed up these many dishes." I said out loud as I entered my kitchen.

"Do you want me to help you out?" Brandon asked as he walked in behind me. Brandy was in his arms rubbing her eyes. Grabbing the Dawn dishwashing liquid, I shook my head at him.

"No thank you. You're helping me out a lot by handling her." I smiled and pointed to Brandy. Brandon laughed and kissed her on the cheek. They walked upstairs, and I got busy cleaning up. Everyone just left with their kids knocked out sleep. We had so much fun and I can't wait for Christmas day. We will be having it at Kelly and Kaylin's house this year and I couldn't wait.

A half an hour later I was done cleaning up the kitchen. I looked in the living room and saw pillows and blankets all on the couch and floor. The kid's blankets were in the corners where they were sleeping at. I waved my hand at that shit. I can tackle that mess tomorrow. I walked back in the kitchen and grabbed a box of popcorn. I wasn't tired yet, so I figured I should catch up on my favorite show. Grabbing the big bowl from on top of the ice box I grabbed my Lays chips to. My popcorn was popping as Brandon walked downstairs. I laughed when I saw his face.

"She gave you a hard time, didn't she?" I asked him laughing. Brandy always gave a hard time when putting her to bed. She didn't cry or anything. She just wanted you to read story after story. All the questions in the would she would decide to ask you right then and there. It was so funny.

"Hell yea, she got that shit from you. All them questions and not taking no for an answer. I read to her twice and even played with her. She finally went to bed when I got in with her and put her on my chest." I laughed as he walked to the hallway to put his boots on. I set the popcorn and chips on the cocktail table in the living room. My TV was turned on to On Demand. I stood in the hallway watching Brandon lace up his boots. He looked up at me before grabbing his coat.

"What'chu about to pig out and watch?" He asked me. I looked in the living room then back at him.

"How to Get Away with Murder. The season has already started, and I haven't watched not one episode." I said to him. He looked at me and nodded slowly. His eyes went from my face to my entire body. I could see his chest go in deep and out slow. I don't know what made me say this, but the words just rolled out.

"Do you wanna watch it with me? You know I can't handle Annalise ass by myself." I did a light laugh. I swear, I never seen Brandon smile as big as he did right now. He rubbed that shit off on me cause now I was cheesing. I watched him take his boots off and follow me into the living room. The fire in the fire place was still lit as we both plopped down on the couch. I grabbed the bag of popcorn and he grabbed the remote. The show was starting, and I looked up at him. He caught me and looked back down at me smiling. I smiled back and started eating popcorn. He put his arm on the back of the couch where I was. We glanced at each other smiling one more time before we put our attention on the TV. Ain't this some shit!

<u>The End</u>

Hey Loves! I hope you guys enjoyed Brandon and Tiff story. I loved writing it and I know ya'll who love Kalvin were ready to kill me lol! I'm not done with my New Orleans men yet. Karlos and Kylee got some shit to say. The will have their own book coming out soon. Thank y'all for rockin' with me and showing me love and support. Love y'all!!
Keep up with me:
Facebook*: www.Facebook.com/LondynLenz*
Instagram: @through_londynlenz
Reading group on Facebook: Through Londyn Lenz

CPSIA information can be obtained
at www.ICGtesting.com
Printed in the USA
LVOW12s2158240118
563853LV00001B/73/P